PENGUIN BOOKS

NIGHT LIGHTS

Author of *California and Other States of Grace* and *Peripheral Visions*, Phyllis Theroux has been a columnist for *Parents* magazine for several years and is a regular contributor to *The New York Times*, *The Washington Post*, and various national magazines. One of the first and most successful writers of *The New York Times*' "Hers" column, she lectures frequently around the country. Theroux lives in Washington, D.C.

*For my children, who have filled my days,
changed my ways, and provided me with much of
the light that continues to illuminate my path.*

NIGHT LIGHTS

✷

BEDTIME STORIES FOR
PARENTS IN THE DARK

✷

Phyllis Theroux

PENGUIN BOOKS

PENGUIN BOOKS

Viking Penguin Inc., 40 West 23rd Street,
New York, New York 10010, U.S.A.
Penguin Books Ltd, 27 Wrights Lane, London W8 5TZ
(Publishing & Editorial) and Harmondsworth,
Middlesex, England (Distribution & Warehouse)
Penguin Books Australia Ltd, Ringwood,
Victoria, Australia
Penguin Books Canada Limited, 2801 John Street,
Markham, Ontario, Canada L3R 1B4
Penguin Books (N.Z.) Ltd, 182–190 Wairau Road,
Auckland 10, New Zealand

First published in the United States of America by
Viking Penguin Inc. 1987
Published in Penguin Books 1988

All but two of the essays in this collection first
appeared, some under different titles, in *Parents
Magazine, The New York Times, The Washington Post*,
and *Family Health*. "Shopping with Children" as
"Shopping as Kids" and "Twentieth Century Jacks" as
"An Old Jill on the Jacks Floor" first appeared in
The Washington Post and are reprinted by permission.
"On Getting Mad," "Capturing the Flag," and the introductory essay
appear here for the first time.

LIBRARY OF CONGRESS CATALOGING IN PUBLICATION DATA
Theroux, Phyllis.
Night Lights.
1. Child rearing—United States—Anecdotes, facetiae,
satire, etc.   2. Parent and child—United States—
Anecdotes, facetiae, satire, etc.   I. Title.
HQ769.T46   1988   649'.1   87-13534
ISBN 0 14 00.8923 3
Printed in the United States of America by
R. R. Donnelley & Sons Company, Harrisonburg, Virginia
Set in Garamond #3 and Antique Roman
Designed by The Sarabande Press

In my dealing with my child, my Latin and Greek,
my accomplishments and my money stead me nothing;
but as much soul as I have avails.
—Ralph Waldo Emerson

ACKNOWLEDGMENTS

The same friends who make it possible for me to move from one day and book to the next are still, thankfully, in place: I am particularly grateful to Judy Diamond, Molly Friedrich, Steven Hofman, Donna Lemert, Willie Warner, Larry and Mary Lou Weisman. I have leaned upon all of the above heavily and they have never complained. Without Jim Gordon, Eve Grimaldi, Agnes Schweitzer, and Robert Spiro, my children would not have prospered half as well. I am further indebted to Elizabeth Crow, at *Parents* magazine, Nan Graham, who loved this book enough to want to publish it, and Robert Massie, who thought of it in the first place.

CONTENTS

~~~~~~

CONTENTS

PART III

NIGHT LIGHTS

INTRODUCTION

~~~~~~

At the end of my freshman year in college, my father telephoned me long distance to deliver some distressing news.
He could no longer afford to keep me there. 1958 had been
a bad year. He had five other children (I was the oldest of
six) to support, and since he had to allocate his resources as
wisely as possible, they would have to be shifted to my next
younger sibling, a brother not yet out of high school.
"Someday," explained my father, "he will be married and
have a family to support."

My father's logic was unassailable. My brother would need
a good education. In the long run, his responsibilities would
be more pressing than mine; I would take my place someday
in another man's family and become part of the responsibilities pressing against him. My father's message was a blow
but I was protected by my own ignorance and a certain
blithe belief that life would support me, perhaps on the
slopes at Aspen, Colorado, where I could spend the next
year skiing, waiting on tables and getting a winter tan.

Fortunately, I did not have to forfeit my college education. At the last minute a scholarship was produced, unso-
licited, by an out-going senior who had heard of my plight,
and donated a large sum of money, enabling me to finish
the next three years with my class. It was a semi-miraculous
reprieve which sobered me. That somebody took me seriously enough to underwrite my education caused me to take

myself more seriously, too. But it would be erroneous to conclude that scholarship money produced a scholar. Like most women of that time I thought in terms of a "vocation," not a career.

A career was, at best, a fill-in occupation between college and marriage, unless you were Margaret Mead or Clare Boothe Luce, whose intellects blazed paths for them which they were then more or less forced to follow. I never thought of myself as being particularly intelligent. Nor, during my entire career at college, was my opinion disputed by any professors there. This did not bother me. I was bent upon being a wife and mother, vocations in which I could not wait to demonstrate the extent of my love, self-sacrifice and purity of intent.

I did, in time, become both a wife and mother. Both vocations do take love, self-sacrifice and purity of intent—more than I have ever had. In more time, I became a single parent, which calls for greater reserves of virtue which I am still searching for. And then—almost without premeditation of any sort—I turned to writing. Writing was a way of creating something, possibly something beautiful or at least beautiful to me, which would be there, unchanged, the next morning for me to continue, like a portrait-in-progress. In the process of becoming a writer, I stumbled upon a career and a slightly altered vision of myself.

Ironically, the brother who received the larger share of my father's purse for the several years that I was on scholarship is a bachelor. In fact, I am still the only one of my parents' six children who has any children to support. Yet here is another irony: my children, while not directly contributing to their own upkeep, have been so continually a direct source of inspiration in the career I eventually pursued, that they have wound up supporting themselves. This collection of essays in which they figure so prominently is proof.

Being the child of a writer who oftentimes writes about her children has been difficult for them at times, although I am a fairly conscientious self-editor, routinely declaring certain aspects of their lives outside the public domain. But as they have grown older and more needful of privacy, I have made it a habit to run anything written about them past their eyes, in case I might have inadvertently violated their lives. On occasion they ask me to delete certain lines. On the whole, however, I think they approve of themselves in print and even take a certain pride in appearing, usually without names, in a newspaper like *The Washington Post* or *The New York Times*—which reminds me of a story I have never had the right place to tell until now.

A long time ago I sat upon my youngest child's bed just before he went off to sleep. The day's events had been reviewed, his prayers had been said, and from his entirely comfortable position in a soft bed with all his teddy bears arranged around his pillow, he blinked sleepily and said, "Now you can sing me a song." His princely imperiousness delighted me. I did what I was told.

Delight was mixed, however, with a certain emptiness of heart about which he knew nothing. A significant part of me ached to be where he was, tucked into bed, drifting off to sleep, while a large, maternal shape perched beside me singing "Sleep, My Child."

While singing, I sorted out the thoughts and feelings which competed for ascendency. Being a parent was, I had discovered, an endlessly demanding profession. At times I could hardly keep my chin up, so exhaustive were the demands. At other times the rewards were extraordinary—the sight, sound and smell of my children were miracle drugs that filled me with euphoria and significance. But here, sitting on the edge of a bed, feeling empty-hearted while filling up the heart of a child who needed a lullaby, was someone who worried that her reserves might run out.

Somewhere between the first and last stanza, I came to a conclusion: It does not matter whether one is at the giving or receiving end of love just as long as one is part of the process in some way. It is only when we become disconnected from the process altogether that we should begin to worry. On that note of hope, I finished singing and kissed my son goodnight.

The next morning I could not help but wonder whether the now fully awake five-year-old at my side had his own thoughts about bedtime. Was he old enough to articulate what it felt like to be fed, bathed, and tucked like a Valentine into an envelope while his mother sang him songs? I decided to ask.

The interview took place while we were driving to the grocery store. Looking over at him, I asked, "Justin, do you remember last night when I was singing you a song?"

"Yep," he answered.

"Do you remember how you felt or what you thought?"

There was a short pause while I assumed he was trying to recollect the moment. Then he looked at me and asked, "Are you doing this for the *Post* or the *Times?*"

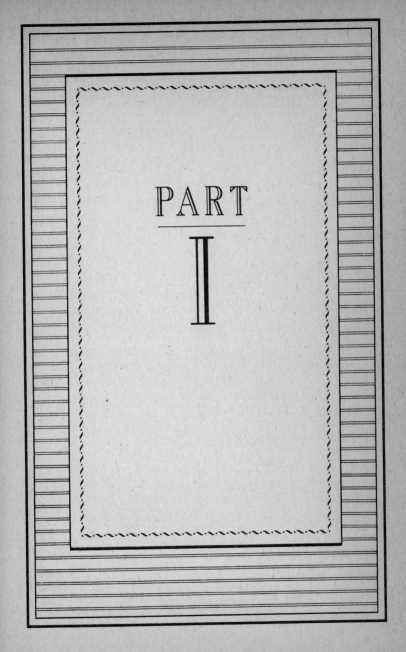

PART
I

BEING BORN

I cannot remember a time when I did not want to have children. This is not to imply that I was anybody's earth mother. As a teenager I loathed baby-sitting jobs, was always trying to get away from my younger brothers and sisters, and I never, as a little girl, played with dolls. But having children was, in my view, a miraculous thing, and it was the miracle I was after.

I should have known better than to chase a miracle so directly. I was married four years and still no children appeared. Looking back, that seems like a rather short period in which to mark time so impatiently, but a marriage without children seemed, to me, like a sandwich with nothing in the middle, and after consulting various doctors, all of whom contradicted each other, I looked up the name of an adoption agency. By that time, how my children arrived seemed far less important than when.

The newborn son whom we adopted in 1967 seemed no less miraculous because I had not produced him myself. Two years later, we adopted a daughter. Together, they entirely eased my maternal ache. Whatever thoughts (and tears) had been produced in me by various doctors who had implied that I was not a child producer disappeared in the presence of children. I was content.

The desire to know what it would be like to bear a child myself resurfaced once when I peered through the maternity-ward window at the newborn daughter of some friends. Emily's eyebrows were a duplicate of her father's—dark, luxuriant and marching straight across the bridge of her infant nose. The miracle of Emily's eyebrows, secretly woven in the chamber of her mother's womb, reactivated an old longing. But it was a fleeting response and I paid it no attention. The demands of raising two toddlers took all the attention I had.

Not long after that visit to the maternity ward, I spent the day with a close friend and confessed that I had been feeling rather depressed without reason. "If I didn't know it wasn't possible, I'd think I was pregnant."

"Oh," she exclaimed, "but you are." My friend Mav is a highly intuitive person who knows a great deal about Carl Jung, dream analysis and Tarot cards. "I didn't mean to shock you," she added, "but I've thought you were pregnant for a while now."

She took out a deck of Tarot cards and asked me to cut the pile. I don't remember how the cards confirmed her intuitive diagnosis but I turned up the death card at least once.

"That's the sign of renewal," she exulted. "I think you ought to go to the doctor and get a rabbit test."

I did. I was. Pregnant. The following week I got the news from the doctor's nurse over the telephone in Mav's kitchen. Both of us cried.

Almost immediately, I felt nauseous when I fried hamburgers. I wore maternity dresses joyfully and long before they were really necessary. I reveled in my condition, made people take photographs of me standing sideways in the garden. I couldn't believe it was happening, but a photograph would not lie. At my tenth college reunion, all my classmates had long since dispensed with childbearing. But

I always was a late bloomer and my late blooming stood out.

Finding the right obstetrician meant changing from the one I had always had. He was tall, elegantly thin and had ice-blue eyes, but I didn't like the way he interrupted our sessions to make golf dates at his country club. He seemed bored with my questions. I worried that when it came time for me to go to the hospital, he would be teeing off on the ninth hole and refuse to answer his beeper. I asked for my file and left.

My second obstetrician was a courtly old Southerner whose reputation—which he confirmed when asked—was for never leaving a pregnant mother's side from the moment she checked into the hospital until the baby was delivered. I thought he was the man for me, except that he told me he had one rule which he never broke: no other men, or husbands, were allowed in the labor or delivery rooms. He didn't think it was healthy for the couple's relationship. Reluctantly I told him that I did not agree with him. The one person I wanted in the delivery room with me, besides the doctor, was my husband. Again, I asked for my file.

Finally I settled on a Cuban who did not promise he would be with me every minute but who approved of fathers participating in the process. He came well recommended, didn't make any golf dates during the first appointment, and was well acquainted with natural-childbirth techniques. He gave me the name of the woman he thought was the best teacher in town.

"She is, how do you say, a little eccentric," he cautioned. "But I think you cannot do better." Her name was Sylvia. Over the telephone, she had a soothing voice. In the seventh month of pregnancy, my husband and I began the Lamaze natural-childbirth course, which she held in her house.

Sylvia lived in a large, crumbling brownstone complex in what was then a downwardly mobile section of Washington, D.C., not far from the White House. It was 1971. The Vietnam war was the explosive issue gripping the nation, and while I was busy painting crib furniture, thousands upon thousands of antiwar protesters were inundating the city—some of them staying at Sylvia's house, as I found out once the classes began.

We met in Sylvia's living room, which was large and oddly furnished with lumpy sofas, fairly clean Indian bedspreads and funny, cobwebbed lamps. Sylvia was a buxom woman in her late thirties with olive skin and thick masses of long, black curly hair that cascaded over her shoulders. At that time she was a nursing mother herself.

At various unannounced intervals, a strapping three-year-old boy, entirely naked, would stride like a lord into the room, throw himself upon his mother's lap, and while Sylvia continued with her lecture ("If you will just imagine the cervix widening the way a sweater neck stretches when you are pulling it over your head"), he would reach up under Sylvia's T-shirt and take possession of a breast.

My husband and I had a little trouble concentrating on the lectures. We weren't the only ones. Arranged around the room were men in sports coats and women in crisp, expandable-front linen dresses who undoubtedly came from sparkling suburban bungalows with pachysandra taking root along the walkways. I don't think any of us had contemplated learning about natural childbirth in such an organic setting. But my unborn child was safely sealed away from the cat hair on the sofa cushions, and I needed the information Sylvia was giving out.

Every so often, Sylvia's husband, or boyfriend (I never bothered to find out his affiliation) would poke his belly through a pair of dusty red velvet curtains which closed off the living room and ask if "Arnie from Detroit" was back from the demonstration yet. Apparently their house was a marchers' crash pad. Sylvia would shake her head and her husband/boyfriend would lazily scratch his stomach and disappear, only to reappear later on to ask if somebody from "The Catonsville Nine" had showed up.

The most remarkable member of the class was the consort of the local Hare Krishna leader. She sat—unattended by her spouse (who did not come for religious reasons)—in the lotus position, in an orange sari, staring sweetly into space. Her lips, which continually mouthed the words "Hare Krishna," moved in rhythm with her fingers, which worked over a set of worry beads in her lap.

Apparently, when her time for delivery came due, she would be attended by various female members of the Hare Krishna community in an upstairs room, while the baby's father chanted downstairs with the men.

Eventually, I got used to the nursing three-year-old, the marcher-paging service and an occasional thud of wet garbage landing on the inside courtyard. Sylvia was a captivating teacher and I eagerly took all the mimeographed sheets on the different stages of labor and transition and read them carefully when I got home.

My husband and I were supposed to practice the various breathing exercises together, pretend to time the contractions and learn how, as a couple, to "birth the baby" as Dr. Lamaze prescribed. But that part of the course never worked. I could never get my husband's attention, I was often tired, and—more importantly—I never quite believed that my pregnancy was real.

Several weeks before the baby was due, I lay in bed looking over the top of my stomach at a television program, filmed in Sweden, on natural childbirth. Up to now, as far as I knew, I had not been apprehensive, but when the baby was pulled out of the mother, a moment which the camera recorded with unobscured fidelity, I surprised myself by involuntarily bursting into tears. Beneath my bravado, I was more frightened than I knew.

The day of delivery arrived. My belief that when the "waters" broke, I would immediately deflate to half my size was the first myth to be disproven. I was admitted to the hospital as bloated as I had been the week before. But as the nurse wheeled me to the labor room, I held my file folder of Lamaze notes in my lap and looked forward to reading them in a quiet, scholarly fashion as the labor progressed. But nature was more violent than I had anticipated.

No sooner had I ensconced myself upon the labor bed than the contractions came with hard, convulsive regularity. All the information from Sylvia's classes jumbled in my head, the notes were flung helter-skelter on the labor-room floor, and for the next eighteen hours, almost without surcease, I was at the mercy of a force which could only be compared to Joseph Conrad's *Typhoon*, where the terrified Orientals traveling in the hold of the boat were flung about like rag dolls in the storm.

"I used to think," said a sophisticated and literary woman friend of mine, "that I was primarily a smart, talky person who was only secondarily a woman. Then I had a baby. I realized it was the other way around." In between contractions, I remembered her words.

My husband did the best he could to make me comfortable, but I was impossible to please. Once, when I flung my arms around his waist as if to save myself from further pain, he joked feebly, "All I can say is 'better you than me.' " I didn't think that was funny at all.

"Where the hell is Dr. García?" I demanded. When he

wasn't in the room, I pictured him stretched out in the nurses' lounge reading a novel. Finally, he came into the labor room once more, and I said, "I'm an old-fashioned girl. Give me everything you've got."

Dr. García smiled, conceded that perhaps twelve hours of hard labor without any anesthesia was as much as I should endure, and ordered an epidural. The first "spinal cocktail" was bliss, the second had no effect, and the third was just beginning to take hold when I was pronounced ready to go into the delivery room. The rest was easy. Within minutes, a very odd, slightly gray-green creature which I could not see very well in the mirrors above my head was eased into the world.

"A boy," said Dr. García pleasantly.

A boy?

It had never occurred to me that a boy was possible. In some unthinking, pre-Columbian way, I could imagine reproducing myself, but it seemed a miracle laid upon miracle to produce an anatomically different human being. As Dr. García expertly sucked fluid out of the tiny mouth of the now slightly pinkish bit of humanity he cradled in his hand, I was suffused with wonder, gratitude and disbelief.

There was some repair work to be done after delivery. I barely noticed. As the doctor stitched and snipped, my husband chatted with him about how his law firm had handled various Cuban expatriates whose money had been confiscated when Castro took over the country.

"Oh, really?" said the doctor, momentarily pausing with his scissors midair. "Maybe I should give you a call."

I would like to say that, back in the labor room, my first memories of holding my son were of him. They were not. My first memory was of being extraordinarily, joyfully hungry, the way one sometimes feels after having made love with someone one loves a great deal. Having had a baby who was so perfect created within me a companion greed for scrambled eggs.

Later on that same morning, with the baby still in transit to the maternity ward, both my husband and I broke down with tears of relief. We had won the Irish Sweepstakes. I don't remember that we ever cried together before . . . or since.

That first night in the hospital, with a desperate need to sleep, I let the baby sleep in the nursery down the hall, but there was one yowling infant who cried continuously all night long. I tossed and turned and tried to find a pocket of drowsiness into which I could sink. But the high, insistent sobs of one baby thwarted all attempts.

Dimly it occurred to me that it might be my child. But it couldn't be. There were over fifteen babies nestled in their plastic containers in the nursery. The odds that the baby was mine were slight. Finally, when I could no longer bear thinking about the possibility, I slid out of bed and walked down the hall. The clock in the hall read 2 A.M. The young nurse on duty in front of the nursery was asleep, her head upon folded arms.

I walked past her, opened the nursery door, and followed the crying to its source. The kicking, disconsolate, sorrowful scrap of humanity in that plastic bassinet was mine. I pulled his crib out of line, wheeled it past the still-sleeping nurse and headed for my room. Just before I pushed him into my room, I glanced back at the nurse, who was now awake and leaning far over her desk to watch my progress, but she did not motion me to return.

"I'm not going to leave you again," I crooned apologetically as I lifted up the tiny, sobbing baby from his bassinet and got into bed with him. "It's all right," I soothed, nestling him against my side. "Don't cry." He gave up one last shudder, as if to say, "I was lost but now am found," and fell asleep.

The next day there was milk in my breasts. I was astonished, not knowing myself, but approving. Visitors came. I feigned matter-of-factness, laughed, made conversation and was—as people had a right to expect—outwardly the same. But I was not the same, and I am still living out the differences. It is difficult to say what those differences are precisely, but they are bone deep.

INSIDE–OUTSIDE

~~~~~~

Once upon a time in my life I was blanketed with babies and desperately willing to label anyone tall enough to reach the doorbell a baby sitter. I contracted with a ten-year-old girl to come to the house every Saturday morning to watch the children. I can't recall what I planned to do with the several hours of free time—often I would sit outside in the car with the doors locked reading a magazine—but the arrangement was, in any event, short-lived.

After several Saturdays on duty, Kathy's face took on a distinctly rumpled look, and one evening she telephoned to confess that she didn't think she would be coming anymore. I had heard that one before, but her reason quite unexpectedly moved me. It wasn't the pay or the children, she explained, but (sigh) "I guess you might say that I'm still more for outside."

Children are, by definition, "more for outside," just as parents are "more for inside," and like many adults I converted from physical to cerebral travel many years ago. It is such a step-saver. Books, the great vitamin supplement of my life, allow me to watch the roast, mind the dog, wait for the plumber and plumb the depths of India with E. M. Forster. But it saddens me to think that my children will remember me as someone who primarily sat at the kitchen table with her nose in a book.

The clearest memory I have of my mother is of a woman

who stood at the stove stirring macaroni and cheese. Is it progress to think I have at least been liberated to the kitchen table? Will my daughter be remembered by her children as someone who lingered on the front steps? Am I Step II in a Vogue pattern? I don't know, but the other day, while worrying with John Updike through one of his metaphysical marriage breakup stories, my usual pattern was altered. My older son ambled into the kitchen and invited me to "play catch." Outside.

My son was nine years old, which is an age that can be summed up as being too old to hold his mother's hand in public unless we're both outside the neighborhood. But he was still quite willing to be seen with me on the block, hands at our sides, and that afternoon he wanted to play catch with me. I was flattered and said yes.

The air was cool, the sun warm, and a late-afternoon quiet had descended on the neighborhood. I felt a little out of uniform in my sling-back shoes and flowered skirt, but no one was looking except my son, whose only interest in me was my performance as receiver. We took up our positions on the street.

Back and forth we shagged the ball—low balls, high balls and bad balls that sent us climbing over fences and searching through bushes. I knew my son was coordinated, but I had not realized just how coordinated. It became incumbent upon me to concentrate just to return his balls in kind.

The concentration paid off. My aim improved. But as I focused more sharply upon the leather missile that sailed in lazy loops through the air, I began to lose my emotional moorings and to feel myself being seduced by a large, untidy world full of trees, grass smells and little twigs that sent the ball bouncing askew when it hit the ground. My consciousness was being rapidly lowered toward the earth. Earth is what you make of it: in the front hall, it must be swept out the door, like children. Outside, it is restored to its original dignity. Again, like children.

A particularly bad ball rolled underneath a parked car. As I got down on my stomach to fish it out from underneath the car's belly, I came eyeball to eyeball with the asphalt. One could do worse than spend a few minutes analyzing asphalt. It has a very interesting texture. And in the brief time that it took me to dislodge the ball, certain antique memories assaulted my mind.

There was a time when I had spent whole years examining asphalt, peeling gum off the sidewalk, studying my ankles for skate-strap abrasions. It was once routine to sit on the front steps and check my knees, which always bore several Africa-shaped scabs in various stages of development. I was also fond of smelling my forearm and pushing around the cartilage at the tip of my nose. There was always something to push, poke or check up on, and I was quite busy in a sidetracked sort of way. But at what moment had single-mindedness entered the picture? When did the cerebral gain ascendency? When did I decide to go inside, never to go outside, for its own sake, in a regular way, again?

Resuming my downwind position on the street, I was suddenly full of forgotten ideas. Maybe after playing catch, the two of us could flatten out a grocery box and slide down the hill behind the school. I tried to remember the rules for "One Foot Off the Gutter." They came back slowly as an ancient information-retrieval system began to reactivate itself. I pictured the two of us roaming around the neighborhood together kicking trash barrels. I hadn't felt so much "for outside" in years.

A particularly fast ball went whizzing by my outstretched hand. "Hah!" rejoiced my son. "Mom just got wasted!"

Perhaps, but nagging in the back of my head was how I might stay outside a little longer. I shot a look at the front door of the house, closed upon the phantom mother who wasn't there. It didn't seem right. Front doors always held mothers behind them, and unless I slipped back inside we would both come kicking through the front door at six-thirty looking for dinner—which would not be there.

The natural division between parents and children reared its work-play head. I looked at my son, idly scratching one ankle with the toe of a sneaker. I knew this was my problem, but it seemed unfair that there was this large outside with only enough room for one of us. Yet that was the case. I had had my chance at the earth and then, quite literally, had risen above it. All that was left for me to do was formulate overviews, which is so very adult.

I sent him the last toss of the afternoon and said, "I have to go inside now . . . dinner." He understood.

PERFECT FAMILIES

~~~~~~

There comes a time in almost all children's lives when they notice that their families are not perfect. With narrowed, resentful eyes, they look out upon the world and realize several things: that life is not fair; that they are leading a low-class, spilled-milk-on-the-floor existence; and that other children of their approximate age, rank and serial number have gotten a better deal. In our family that time is now.

To begin with, my children receive so few goods and services in comparison with other, more fortunate friends. Sarah's mother always serves Sarah fresh orange juice before she has even tumbled out of her canopy bed in the morning. Georgette is driven to school (no public transportation for her) in a car that talks.

"Talks?" I asked my thirteen-year-old daughter, who was slumped in the front of our six-year-old generic-brand sedan with plastic seat covers.

"Yes," she hissed accusingly. "When the door isn't shut a computer says, 'Your door is ajar.'"

My daughter then went on to describe Georgette's mother, who never leaves the house without wearing something searingly appropriate—like a pair of champagne-color twill slacks with a silk blouse and a matching blazer. How a mother looks is crucially important to a child.

I remember one cold winter's day, telephoning my daughter at a friend's house and asking if she wanted me to give her a ride home. There was a pause at the other end of the line. Finally she asked, "What are you wearing?" In perfect families, mothers are always dressed for success.

The families my children admire and envy have houses where the rugs have fresh vacuum tracks on the surfaces, the air smells like chocolate-chip cookies, and the kitchens are full of appliances one finds only in the suburb of a fully developed country: "Mr. Coffee" machines, microwave ovens, intercoms, maids. A maid, of course, is a human being, not an appliance, but she does keep them polished, and after extolling the virtues of his best friend's house of impeccable condition my twelve-year-old son did admit, "Well, they *do* have a maid who comes three times a week."

"Aha," I exclaimed, "so that explains why their house always looks so beautiful."

"Yes," he said, "but Mrs. Flannery has standards, and we don't."

That was a punch-line below the belt, reminding me of the time I gave instructions to a maid whom I had temporarily employed: "Louise, you are not here to maintain my standards. You are here to *raise* them." Louise did not last very long.

In time, all children discover that tidy families with tidy incomes are not, ipso facto, the happiest of units. If my children stopped at these materialistic comparisons, I would be able to hold my own. But my children's sharp eyes for perfection have located other families whose merits I can neither dismiss nor imitate so easily. These are the outrageously happy families. "I know the type," said one friend. "They force bulbs in the winter, and they always bloom."

Outrageously happy families always seem to be living out a perpetual punch line. They laugh, joke and tell funny stories about each other in the kitchen. When you are in their presence, you get intoxicated with the possibilities of interrelatedness. The Westons (whose name, like all the others, has been changed to preserve their innocence) are a case in point.

"I can't explain it," said my daughter solemnly. "But they are just so funny." The funereal look on her face was in sharp contrast to her story. "Even their dogs—and they have three, Mom, not just one like us—are funny . . . and their Christmas tree."

"Their Christmas tree is funny?"

"Yeah, it's all scraggly, and the Westons make jokes about it."

You can't win with funny families. They make you feel as if your own family is a chain gang linked by grim, unbreakable circumstances. To be accused of heading up a family that doesn't have any fun is to feel a sword in my heart. Fun ought to be something I should be able to produce, like a deck of cards, by the fire on a snowy night.

Of course, a parent often feels like a stage director who can't get all the characters on stage to read their lines properly. Somebody is out, somebody else is sulking, and the third person has just burned the popcorn pot and refuses to clean it up. In perfect families, these things may happen but everybody laughs.

I encountered my first "perfect family" when I was in the sixth grade. It belonged to Rebecca and—even if she had declared herself an orphan—I would have gladly paid cash for the honor of being her best friend. For a few months, before my term was up, I held that honor. There was nothing about Rebecca that I did not like.

She was slim, smart and compassionate. She always had better ideas than the rest of us, who always executed them upon command. I was an avid reader of books in which heroines like Rebecca led slightly perilous lives that called all their virtues into play. I saw Rebecca as a heroine without traumas. She had everything, including a family that would guarantee her, I assumed, a life free of complications until she died.

The house she lived in was a large, ivy-covered brick mansion which looked rather like the dorm of an Ivy League college. Rebecca had a fireplace in her bedroom. I had never thought of a fireplace in a bedroom before. It was an elegant idea.

Rebecca's parents were rich but friendly. Her sisters were blond or brunette duplicates of her—full of high color and style. As a family, they were always doing photogenic things, like going to Sun Valley for the holidays or raking up autumn leaves in kilts while Rebecca's mother made hot chocolate in the kitchen. I never spent any time at Rebecca's house without wishing I could change places with her. But families cannot be switched like sweaters, just because the one you're wearing itches. I always felt enormously frustrated when I returned home.

This is not to say that I did not love my own family. But at the age of twelve, my love was a silent underground river flowing beneath my conscious thoughts. After a weekend at Rebecca's house, I came home and saw only squalling babies, fingerprints on the walls and a brother who slurped his cereal until I wanted to crack the bowl over his head. I belonged to a family that was tacky, albeit intact.

Two years after I met Rebecca, her parents divorced for reasons that are too seamy to go into. The "perfect family" scattered. Rebecca's mother eventually remarried but was killed in a car crash at the other side of the country. Since then, I have lost touch completely with my old sixth-grade friend. But when somebody first whispered in my ear about the divorce, I remember weeping with outrage and sorrow.

The emotion was at least twofold—for Rebecca, whom the gods in their mercy ought to have bypassed—and for myself, whose vision of a perfect family was destroyed.

There are, however, certain families that demand an even higher level of philosophizing. They are, quite simply, fortunate. For reasons of luck, karma, metabolism or a combination, they walk in brighter sunshine than other families. How does one relate to these kinds of families? How do you divert envy into a positive emotion? Do these healthy, two-parent, reasonably well off and productive families have any relation to us?

Parents, needless to say, are not immune from envy any more than their children are. We just tend to hide it better. As a single parent I have had dark moments when I have gazed at my three children and wished they had been endowed with more of everything—including at least one adult who knows how to kick the show into shape.

Envy, however, can be deadly. To envy is to draw circles that isolate us from others, to take small, bitter trips that diminish the traveler. Better, I think, to view fortunate families the way audiences view graceful dancers or singers—with appreciation. Children should feel enlarged, not threatened, by somebody else's life. As for my own children, I am beginning to see that their adversities have made them more understanding of others. With less than everything they need, they are developing a generosity of mind.

The other day my son, sixteen, said he had almost given his new jacket to a man on the street who didn't have one. "I figured that if I had one good jacket and he had none that I could get another while he couldn't." He didn't quite succumb to the impulse, but the right connections were in place.

The middle child, now fourteen, has developed a better sense of humor despite what she calls our "lack of facilities." At night when I rub her back and she temporarily stops hating me, she counsels me to "hang on" until she's twenty. "Why twenty?" I asked her. "Because by then I'll be in a more intellectual phase," she replied.

The youngest, still caught up with the ideal of perfect families, is too philosophical to be caught up with them forever. Which is not to say that I don't get my daily instructions on how to improve.

The first afternoon that he asked his new best friend (of the beautiful house) to come over to play, he begged me to have everything in order. When he came home, the house shone like a waxed apple in a blue bowl on a gingham tablecloth. He did not show any visible signs of relief but when his friend wasn't looking he gave me a circle of approval with his thumb and index finger. Before going to sleep he was more eloquent: " . . . and you even fixed the windowpane on the front door."

"That's because I'm a perfect mother who wants to give her son a perfect house to show off," I replied.

"Well, forget that," he said. "You're not the type."

I dove for his rib cage beneath the blankets and started to tickle him in mock retaliation. "I may not be perfect, but what you see is what you get."

He was too busy laughing to forge a snappy comeback. But for one moment, we were a family with a high level of interrelatedness. I envied no one at all.

ON BEING FAIR

When I was young, television was still so primitive that I had no chance to ruin my intellect unless I wanted to watch "Howdy Doody" through a blizzard of interference. For want of a recreational alternative, I usually sulked or read books. There was a connection. I sulked because I felt victimized by unfair circumstances, and the books I read while sulking revolved around heroines whose lives were stacked against similar odds.

Looking back, the parents or guardians of these heroines were invariably shadow figures. There was no suggestion of parental influence on children, all of whom were more or less immaculately conceived. But in real life, parents do influence their children and I often wonder whether my sins will be transferred, my strengths adopted; or am I only a shadow figure in my children's lives who should not overestimate my own influence? I suspect the answer to all of the above questions is "Yes." But midway through the parenting process I know one thing absolutely. A wonderful parent is, above all, fair.

Children are wired for fairness almost from infancy. Watch how carefully they keep an eye on the glasses when you are pouring lemonade. A millimeter more lemonade in Daphne's glass will cause her brother, Schuyler, to wail over the injustice of the proportions, as if they were a direct reflection of how you really felt about him. As for little Daphne, silently drinking her lemonade, she obviously considers more her just due.

I have never known a child who wasn't capable of receiving extra love, attention or toys without feeling guilty; all children consider themselves equal under the law unless the balance shifts their way. But should they receive less, their faces become torches of righteousness, and, with all the moral energy they possess, they cry "Foul!"

For years I tried to be the fair parent my children needed me to be. A new bicycle for the oldest meant, ipso facto, that I was committing myself to the purchase of two more bikes down the road. If I spent an extra half hour saying goodnight to one child, the other two would demand equal time, and, of course, I gave it to them. God forbid that any of my children should think I was discriminating against them, even though I was.

Parents of only children have, I assume, an easier time on the fairness front. Abused or cossetted, an only child has no other sibling to use as a measuring rod. But when there are three children and, in my case, one parent who must waltz between them parceling out privileges, chores and attention, the chances for them to wail "That's not fair!" are endless. And for a long time I just stood there unable to defend myself. The fact of the matter is that I was (and am) unfair most of the time.

Take language. The oldest child, a boy, used to split the air routinely with expletives. I would try in various ways (including packing his trunk and leaving it by the front door) to let him know that I could not tolerate his behavior. Very little worked except the maturing process—his, not mine.

The middle child, a girl, is much more soft-spoken.

Whenever she tried to match her older brother's verbal pyrotechnics I was all over her like a candle snuffer.

The youngest, another boy, uses rotten language on occasion—usually because he can see no other way to enlarge his position. I am more tolerant of his cursing than of his older sister's, but less tolerant than I am with his older brother. How, one has the right to ask, can a parent justify behaving in such an inconsistent way?

Here is how. The eldest, beneath his macho veneer, used to be the least secure emotionally. He simultaneously needed more control and more freedom than the other two children. There were times when I simply pretended that I could not hear him, knowing that he needed to let off steam.

My middle child, frankly, was always easier for me to intimidate. I expected more of her—the fate of a child who has always given me every reason to expect that she would not let me down. Then, too, I am not yet acclimated to the present-day unisex vocabulary. Cursing sounds worse from girls.

As for the youngest child, he rarely lapsed, and it sounded so ridiculous when he tried to "talk tough" that a part of me did not believe what my ears heard.

These were my reasons. To some extent, they still are. But only recently have I felt more comfortable with this sort of wishy-washy, "ad hoc" parental behavior—perhaps because I have begun to know my own limits and to be more comfortable with myself.

Many times I have longed for a personality transplant. My first choice would be to become the Marine drill sergeant played by Lou Gossett, Jr., in *An Officer and a Gentleman*. My children have needed Lou Gossett from the start. Instead they must limp along with somebody who often resembles Laura in *The Glass Menagerie*.

Easily thwarted or fooled, guilt-ridden and absent-minded, I can't even remember what rules I made for watching television last week, let alone enforce them. But, like most parents, I do have an up-to-date file on each of my children. I more or less know, psychologically, where they are at any given time.

Thus, I judge that one child needs more of me at bedtime, perhaps for a week running. And I give it to him without feeling I must account for it to the others. With all three children legitimately clamoring for new clothes, I decide to give the entire month's clothes budget (not that I actually have one) to my daughter. She has done poorly on a history exam; her best friend has moved; and I have been very busy. Buying her some clothes gives her a chance to rebuild her esteem and me a chance to rebuild our relationship. The boys wait, even though "it's not fair."

Lest one should get the incorrect impression that this particular parent is a model of "enlightened unfairness," it seems important to stop here and admit that there is nothing enlightened about neglect, inappropriate responses or ignorance—all of which are part of my parental resumé. But while it is often said, in defense of children, that they flounder because childhood itself is a new experience, parents have never before experienced parenthood either. In fairness, that ought to be pointed out.

Mistakes are the usual bridge between inexperience and wisdom, and on more than one occasion I have taken my children aside and sincerely apologized for having treated them unfairly. But the unfairness I have apologized for is not the short-term "you-did-the-dishes-twice-he-didn't-do-them-at-all" variety. It is the long-term unfairness, usually born of insensitivity, for which I try to make amends.

Oddly, when I sincerely ask forgiveness from my children, they are extraordinarily lenient. They make excuses for my behavior or deny it altogether. But somehow a rift is healed, and my acknowledging that I have been wrong gives them the idea that being wrong is not the worst thing that can happen. Life does go on.

That being said, I don't think a parent can be fair and sane simultaneously. There is too much bookkeeping involved. If Jack's blue jeans cost $23.95 and you only got Jill a $13 shirt, then that means you owe Jill . . . There would be no end to the balancing act a parent would have to perform.

Then, too, rearing three children is like growing a cactus, a gardenia and a tubful of impatiens. Each needs varying amounts of water, sunlight and pruning. Were I to be absolutely fair, I would have to treat each child as if he or she were absolutely identical to the other siblings, and there would be no profit for anyone in that.

The other afternoon, for example, my daughter tried to pry out a later-than-usual curfew for a weekend evening. Being unsuccessful, she resorted to accusing me of being a hypocrite—after all, her older brother was allowed to stay out later when he was her age.

She was right. I had allowed him to stay out later, a permission I would not have given him if I knew then what I know now. But I did not mention this to her.

"Do you think that you're different from your brother?" I asked her.

My daughter is no dummy. She could see the corner I was constructing for her. How many times had she told me that she certainly was *not* like her brother, the implication being that she had more class.

"No . . . well, yes," she replied.

"Well, of course you're different," I confirmed, ignoring

the first half of her answer. "And that's why I treat you differently. Otherwise, it wouldn't be fair."

I hated myself for being so manipulative. But when one is trying to raise children, sometimes foul is fair.

TEN-YEAR-OLDS
TACKLE FOOTBALL

When the world was new and I was operating under the misperception that the child who wears a seersucker jacket will stay out of jail, I used to wheel my infant son routinely past the local football field and be shocked at what I saw.

There, running their feet off in terrorized precision, was a team of small boys, under the command of a latent Nazi who puffed Marlboros and strode up and down the sidelines hurling insults: "Get the lead out of your drawers, Rafferty," and, "I want power from you, Number Forty-four, do you hear that? *Power!*"

My little son, whose ears were accustomed to "Songs from Mister Rogers" on the phonograph and the soft crunch of zwieback in his crib, would gaze inquiringly in the direction of these new sounds. "What's the matter with you, Alvarez?" yelled the coach, shaking the stick he rapped helmets with. "Did you eat marshmallows for breakfast, or what?"

Or what, indeed! Clenching my fingers around the handle of the stroller where my baby son was nestled in his Best & Company snowsuit, I would mutter, "Oh, no, he's not going to get his hands on you." And wheeling the Infant of Prague home, I spun my dreams of male evolution over the babybonneted head of the child who would be a flute player or possibly a forest ranger who cared about all the tiny things in the woods.

Well, ten years is ten years. A lot has transpired, as they say. Best & Company has gone out of business; I can't even remember what a seersucker jacket looks like; and my son—who tends to view tiny things in the woods as objects to hurl through windows if only he can perfect his aim—is no longer a Lilliputian. A ten-year-old boy can go one of two ways: to the top of the class or to the bottom of the heap. This September I found myself on the very same football field, plucking at the sleeve of the very same coach, begging him to accept my son on the 75-pounder football team and to run his legs off until it was too dark to see the field.

I believe this is what is known as capitulating. Or, to put it another way, what we most earnestly run from tends to be standing at the far end of the field, smoking Marlboros and waiting for us to sign up. Nor was I the only capitulator on the field. There were other parents on this first day of the football season who were chatting up Coach Burkhead and plunking down a dollar for dues—all for the privilege of enlisting their sons in the school of hard, even violent, knocks.

Why? Were we not all graduates of "Sesame Street"? Did we not know that football was the sport of animals? Yes, to both questions. But the question of hurling rocks at streetlamps and teasing Officer Friendly in an unfriendly way was submerged in those Rubber Duckie days. Energy in a pre-adolescent can either flow laterally across a football field or down the drain. But looking at the small boy struggling to pull a jersey (dear God, why Number 13?) over enough plastic parts to roof a stegosaurus, I realized that Number

13 was not burdened with these parental nightmares. Why was my son drawn to this kidney-smasher of a sport?

Certain questions are difficult to research. Children are tight-lipped about what moves them emotionally, and when I eased up to the drinking fountain to try to overhear the pep talks that inspired my son to get up at 5:30 A.M. and rub cleanser on his helmet, he sent such dark stares in my direction that I was forced to back off. But not before I had caught some of the magic of the game.

There was no doubt in my mind that Coach Burkhead viewed my child as a piece of meat with legs. Mothers were the chauffeurs who transported the meat to the field. But as I bent over the drinking fountain and eavesdropped over the spume, it became obvious that while Coach Burkhead was not "into" mothers, he knew every kid on the team—not only by name, but by heart.

"Robbie," he called out, pulling at one boy's helmet affectionately as he strode by him, "you did good today—made their quarterback look like a flower arranger out there. I'm proud of you. Put an Ace bandage on your ankle when you get home."

"But Stephen—where are you, Stephen? Listen, you want to know why you didn't play today? Well, I'll tell you. You didn't show up on time for practice on Friday and you still haven't learned to quit putting the blame on some other teammate for things that go wrong."

A small, tentative excuse whimpered down the bleachers from a kid with an expensive haircut. Burkhead cut him off.

"This is a team, Stephen. Everybody pulls together or we fall on our face. And I don't want to hear any more stuff about getting out late from the orthodontist. One more late show on the field and you're off the team."

With that rejoinder, Burkhead was back to business,

demonstrating plays, moving around imaginary team members and punching the air as he explained how, in the second half, they could tighten up a loose end. Not one boy fidgeted. Not one boy fooled around. Such rapt, mystical expressions have not been seen since *Star Wars* left town. Every member of the 75-pounder team gazed with serious adoration at the same man who, only ten years ago, I thought ought to be arrested for child abuse. By the end of the pep talk, the boys were thrilled to the soles of their "Juice Mobile" cleats and clattered down onto the field imbued with purpose, ready for the opposing team, who, it was strongly rumored, wore razor blades in their kneepads.

They say that courage is first learned on the fields of our youth, that the will to overcome the odds of wearing a Number 13 jersey is provided by men like Coach Burkhead. Would that the game were badminton. Would that football, pitting human beings against each other on either side of a scrimmage line, did not resemble, too closely for my comfort, war.

But life is not a badminton game. Even children know that. What they also know but would rather be benched for all eternity than actually admit is that they love Coach Burkhead. And what Coach Burkhead knows, but is too busy blocking out plays and telling kids not to goof off en route from the orthodontist, is that the feeling is mutual. The most obvious thing, however, is mentioned not at all. Small boys learn to be large men in the presence of large men who care about small boys.

SHOPPING
WITH CHILDREN

~~~~~~~~~~~~~~~~~~~~~~~~~~~~~~~~~~~~~~

Once upon a time there were three little children. By and large, dressing them was a joyful thing. At a moment's notice, their mother could turn the boys into baby Rothschilds, the girl into a shipping heiress, or even a Kennedy. In those early days of motherhood, I used to take a lot of photographs for the scrapbook. Now I flip through the scrapbook sometimes to remind myself that "those were the days."

The eldest son was the first to establish his individuality: sleeveless Army jackets, kneecap bandannas and a pierced ear hidden under a lengthening hair style. Then the youngest son discovered dirt. He formed a club, still active, called "The All Dirt Association." To qualify, one had to roll in the mud.

Fortunately, the little girl grows increasingly more tasteful and immaculate. She will get up at 5:30 A.M. to make sure she has enough time to wash and curl her hair so that it bounces properly on her shoulders when she goes off to school, and she screams as if bitten by an adder if a drop of spaghetti sauce lands on her Izod. The entire house is thrown into an uproar while she races for the Clorox bottle. This is a family of extremists, and nobody dresses for the kind of success I had in mind.

Time will tell what happens to these children. Who can say whether my son the dirt bomb will wind up sewing buttons on a seersucker sports jacket, or my daughter the Southamptonian will discover the joys of thrift-shop browsing. They are still evolving toward personal statements that are, at this writing, incomplete.

In the meantime, however, they must be dressed, which means taking them to stores where clothing for their growing bodies can be purchased. Shopping with children is exactly as awful as shopping with parents. But if the experience is to be survived there are certain rules all adults must follow. (If you are a child, you may not read any further. This is for your parents, who will deal with you very harshly if you read one more word!)

RULE I: Never shop with more than one child at a time. This rule is closely related to another rule—never raise more than one child at a time. If you understand the second rule, there is no need to elaborate upon the first.

RULE II: Dress very nicely yourself. After the age of nine, children do not like to be seen with their mothers in public. You are a blot upon their reputation, a shadow they want to shake. I, myself, always insisted that my mother walk ten paces behind me, take separate elevators and escalators and speak only when spoken to—which brings me to the next rule.

RULE III: Do not make any sudden gestures, loud noises or heartfelt exclamations such as "How adorable you look in that!" or "Twenty-nine ninety-five! Are you kidding? For a shirt?" Children are terribly embarrassed by our eccentricities, and it goes without saying that you must never buy their articles of "intimate apparel" in their presence. Children, until enough sleazy adults teach them that it is old-fashioned, are very modest creatures. One time I ran out of the store and took the bus home by myself after my mother asked a salesclerk where the "underpants" counter was. Everyone in the store heard her. I had no choice.

RULE IV: Know your child's limits. If he can be coerced into a department store, coaxed into telling you that he wouldn't mind wearing this shirt or that pair of pants, don't insist that he go the whole distance—i.e., don't force him to try them on. Keep the sales slips; if something doesn't fit when he tries it on at home, return it. If he cannot be made to enter the store at all, say, "Fine. When you run out of clothes, wear your sister's." Children who won't go shopping at all save their parents a lot of time.

RULE V: Know your own limits. Do not be dragged to every sneaker store in the metropolitan area to find the exact shoes your child has in mind. Announce: "We're going to Sears—and Sears only—unless you want to wait for six more weeks, which is the next time I am free." Some children, with nothing but time and a passion to improve their image, will cheerfully go to three stores they know about and six more they don't, without blinking an eye.

RULE VI: Keep your hand on your checkbook. This is a very hard rule to follow if you are not strong-minded. Children can accuse you of ruining their lives because you do not genuflect before the entire line of Ocean Pacific sportswear, and girls have a way of filling you with guilt by telling you that every other girl in their confirmation class is going to be wearing Capezio sandals and if you want to make her look funny in front of the bishop she will never forgive you as long as she lives.

RULE VII: Keep on top of the laundry. Or, if you can't keep on top of the laundry, remember that the wardrobe your son or daughter wants is probably lying in the bottom of a hamper waiting to be retrieved. When packing a trunk for camp or school, insist that everything the child owns be washed (preferably by him or her), folded and ready to be inventoried before you go to the store to fill in the gaps. Your children will hate you for enforcing this rule, but remember that true love is strong.

RULE VIII: Avoid designer clothes. Shut your eyes to labels. Do not be intimidated by the "fact" that your daughter cannot go to the movies without swinging a Bermuda Bag, or that your son will not be able to concentrate in the library without Topsiders on his feet. Tell your children that the best thing about Gloria Vanderbilt is her bank account, fattened by socially insecure people which, thank God, they are not!

Having laid down the rules, it is important to refresh the adult's memory with "remembrances of things past." I have never met a child who did not remind me of how difficult it is to present a confident face to the world. Clothing is only the top blanket shielding them from the elements, and children need all the protective covering they can get.

As a child, I knew in an inarticulate way that I stood a better chance of surviving a windstorm in a circle of trees. My aim was to be the tree in the middle, identical and interchangeable with every other sapling in the grove. How I dressed had everything to do with feeling socially acceptable and when I inadvertently slipped into an individualism I could not back up with sustained confidence, I would try to think what I could do to regain my place in the grove.

It seemed to me that social success depended on having at least one of three commodities: a fabulous personality, fame, or a yellow Pandora sweater. These were the building blocks upon which one could stand.

A fabulous personality was beyond my power to sustain on a daily basis. Fame, like lightning, seemed to strike other people, none of whom I even knew. But a yellow Pandora sweater could be purchased at Macy's, if only my mother would understand its cosmic importance. Fortunately, she did.

For several days, or as long as it took for the sweater cuffs to lose their elasticity, I faced the world feeling buttoned up, yellow and self-confident—almost as confident as Susan Figel, who had a whole drawerful of Pandora sweaters in different shades to match her moods.

Unfortunately, I remember that yellow Pandora sweater a little too vividly. When I am shopping with my children, empathy continually blows me off course in the aisles. On the one hand, nobody wants her child to look funny in front of the bishop. On the other, it has yet to occur to my children that the bishop in full regalia looks pretty funny himself.

JOHANNA'S FIRST DAY AT SCHOOL

It is popular, because it is convenient, to operate on the notion that there are no real differences between children and adults. Flesh is flesh, blood is blood, and terror—whether you are nine or ninety—sends adrenaline racing through the body. All this is true. But children have one disadvantage: in the face of fear they don't know how to "fake it." I have yet to see a nine-year-old getting ready for the first day of school who isn't awash in vulnerability. As she stands before the hall mirror adjusting the ponytail with panicked fingers that can't get the rubber band around the tail, she knows she looks all wrong.

The first day of school is a terrifying ritual, no matter how many times September has rolled around. And while it torments the life of every child, grownups tend to discount this terror. I don't.

The first day of school is a test of enormous magnitude. The child must, quite literally, step over a threshold, confront a classroom teeming with brawling, semiformed egos and somehow scrape through the day with as much dignity as possible.

The hope is that last June's bosom-buddy-lifelong-friend-and-pal will have been faithful to your memory. The fear is

that over the summer some mysterious realignment of loy-
alties may have been formed. And while during the summer
a child can lay aside his shield and bivouac in the backyard
with no worries about who will be his partner at recess, old
worries get resurrected in the fall.

I used to dread the first day of school because I knew that
even if I was a roaring success I wouldn't have the psychic
energy to maintain the momentum for the rest of the year.
There weren't enough eggs in the soufflé of my personality
to hold the whole thing up. I could fake the first day, but
not the second, third and twenty-fourth.

Last September, the children in this house reacted pre-
dictably. They chose the socks guaranteed to hold their elastic, shoes that were as chic as possible, the best pants and
the absolutely right jump suit. There was much jockeying
before the mirror as they tried to comb themselves into the
sort of conformity that would make them acceptable. The
point was to look perfect, but conventional—like a child
model in the Sears catalog. I understood this instinct. After
all, their lives were on the line.

The preliminaries accomplished, they waved goodbye from
the front porch, new lunch boxes twinkling in the morning
sun. I uttered my usual prayer, that they would be all right.
Then, since even mothers have other things on their mind
besides their children, I forgot about the first day of school
until I drove up to retrieve them at 3 P.M.

Dozens of little boys and girls were clambering about the
front steps, laughing, shouting and acting as if the first day
of school had been a figment of their imagination. Yet, as I
stood waiting for my own children to emerge from the
building, my eye was caught by one little girl for whom
the first day of school was a triumph of self-confidence over
the odds.

In my daughter's fourth-grade class there are fifteen girls.

With the exception of Johanna, they are all fairly desperate to be exactly like every little girl there. But that is not possible for Johanna. She is, first of all, twenty pounds heavier than anyone else in the class. She is taller, biracial, adopted, and neither brilliant nor a joke teller. Circumstances have come together to make her different, and Johanna might have crept into school on the first day, looking neither left nor right, hoping that all these strikes would not be held against her. She did no such thing.

Johanna stood on the school steps like a self-satisfied princess, wearing a long pink nylon dress—one of her mother's nightgowns—tied around the waist with a wide piece of pink satin blanket binding. She had chosen to wear over her nightgown-dress—rightly so, I thought—a white knitted cape with a tasseled fringe. Then, since one always needs accessories, to complement the main idea, she had found a bright-pink plastic headband with an eternally perky pink bow to set on top of her dark-brown curly hair. Johanna stood out on the front steps like a peony among tweed suits.

I watched Johanna and read on her face a look of satisfaction that was neither arrogant nor silly. The fact is that Johanna looked absolutely ravishing. I knew it. She knew it. Everybody knew it. But what nobody, perhaps not even Johanna, knew is how she acquired the advanced understanding that enabled her to convert a hazardous mine field into a tour de force.

Johanna had turned the first day of school on its ear. May her mother never run out of nightgowns. May Johanna never run out of steam.

TO MANNERS BORN

One of the hallmarks of the "good child" is good manners. The child we want to know and be around is polite, without being a goody-goody about it; understands that adults don't like to be interrupted mid-conversational stream; and cheerfully volunteers (ideally, without being asked) to rush to the kitchen to refill the water pitcher when it runs dry at the dining-room table. I have known children like this and wondered whether there wasn't a woodshed somewhere behind their house where the parents routinely whipped them with cat o' nine tails into the sweet submission I witnessed in their living rooms. Teaching children manners is a difficult task.

My own children initially approached the subject of manners the way one might approach a plate of unsalted spinach. They understood the principle involved but saw no reason why they had to absorb it. It was a principle of mine, not theirs, and none of their friends' parents demanded that they shoot up from the sofa to shake hands when a guest entered the room.

Each adult has his or her own standards, those limits beyond which they cannot bear their children to go, as far as being polite (or impolite) is concerned. I seem pre-programmed for demanding that my children immediately rise with a pleasant welcoming expression on their faces when a neighbor or friend of mine comes to visit. I even demand that other people's children, when they are in my house, behave in the same way.

If they persist in remaining in the lounge position, I will lift them bodily upward, or orally request that they lift themselves up—which my children find justifiably embarrassing. But they have learned that the best way to avoid being embarrassed is to jump like a frog off a hot rock whenever a visitor who is not the meter reader from the gas company comes into the house.

I have just begun this small conversation on manners from strength. Naturally, my children—now familiar with the cattle prod I figuratively hold in my hand—respond correctly, although there were a number of years when I was far more lax about the fine points of this rule.

Should a child, en route to the kitchen, be expected to halt and say "Hello, Mr. Warner, how are you?" or is it acceptable to keep on pushing toward the refrigerator without so much as a sidelong glance into the living room? Usually I would be so engaged by the conversation between Mr. Warner and myself that I did not notice the lack of acknowledgment. Then I realized that my friends took it rather amiss when they were slighted. Nobody likes to feel that he does not exist, or worse, is perhaps considered an intrusive element in somebody else's home.

Now I have my children trained to divert their steps from the kitchen or front door with a small greeting and a polite question or two aimed toward the guest ensconced in the wing chair. There has been a very positive payoff here. The guests are usually full of compliments for the children, compliments I pass on to them after the guest has left.

One of the subconscious beliefs that most children have,

in my experience, is that they are invisible to adults—which adults often reinforce. Politeness is a two-way street. But when it is pointed out that even adults can get their feelings hurt, this can shock children into realizing that they have an unexpected impact upon "grownups." Perhaps they are not as invisible as they had thought.

Now for my weaknesses in the manners department: The one that looms largest in my mind is "thank you notes." Every Christmas, after the presents from various godparents and grandparents have been unwrapped and appreciated, I vow that this year we will not celebrate the New Year before all three children have written a thank you note for each present they had received. I seem to remember that there was one Christmas when that vow became a reality. Only one.

Sitting all three children down at the dining-room table after supper, I passed out stationery and pens for the project. The wailing was immediate. "I don't know how to write a letter," "I'm missing a Charlie Brown special *right now*," "I'll do it tomorrow," "I didn't even like the present!" Most of the evening was spent trying to keep three small bottoms pressed onto three chairs as I lashed them into compliance. The effort was so tremendous on my part that for the next several Christmases I resorted to fecklessly inquiring whether this child or that one had written to Aunt Anne Marie, knowing full well that their muffled answers were all variations on the word "no."

What this teaches children, of course, is that all presents are acceptable but that acknowledgment is not necessary. It further teaches them to think no further than the wrapping paper. Never mind that Mrs. Clark spent a considerable amount of time shopping in a crowded department store for "the right thing" for a ten-year-old boy, bought it, wrapped it, and made a trip to the post office to send it off. These details of Mrs. Clark's life are not important. Or so the parent who does not insist upon thank you notes implies without words.

That lesson was brought home to me, on an adult level, last June when I gave a shower for a woman who was getting married. Granted, I had received a great deal of pleasure rounding up the silver service, filling the house with flowers, and anticipating the look of happiness on her face as she sat surrounded by presents. In advance of the event, I was rewarded well.

But several weeks later a small bell went off in my head. Without exactly looking for it, I had expected a letter in my mailbox from the bride-to-be saying *something* about how nice the afternoon had been. It has not come to this day. I am not prepared to shove her into a stone wall and batter her if and when I bump into her in the street in the future. But I do intend to say something. And saying something— of a positive note—is what thank you notes, even for the youngest of children, is all about.

The list of gifts received and unacknowledged in this house is not too long and too many years old for me to set straight. How many dolls, sweaters, and dresses currently being played with, or worn, or passed on, have remained unacknowledged I no longer know. But next Christmas, I intend to revert to the "here we all are at the dining-room table and nobody's leaving until all people have been thanked in writing" method of manners enforcement. It seems to be the only way to handle the issue well.

Of course, not all thank you notes are exactly what the parent supervising the process had in mind. I recall one that I probably should have censored before it left the house, but I hoped the recipients would allow for the age (nine) and candor of the writer and understand the spirit in which it was sent. They did.

DEAR CHRIS AND BUNNY,

Thank you for the headphone radio. The only problem is it only gets A.M. But thanks anyway.

Your godson,
JUSTIN

THE BOREDOM FACTOR

~~~~~~~~~~~~~~~~~~~~~~~~~~~~~~~~~~~~

Childhood's Worst Disease

When I was a child, I had two resources at my immediate disposal: time and my mother. When time hung too heavily on my hands, I would push, pull and bump up against my mother like a pinball machine. "What," I would ask, "can I do?"

Invariably my mother would suggest unacceptable alternatives to my boredom, like cleaning up my room or reading a book, which seemed like curing a virus with a virus. I wanted action, drama, the cutting edge of life's knife to get me through the day.

One evening I poured ketchup over myself and pretended to be dead in the bathtub. On another occasion I faked a polio attack. Once I took a can of paint and drew a long green stripe across everybody's house front on the block. Boredom is the devil's tool.

These were not fruitful occupations, and I do not suggest them to my own children, who now use me like a pinball machine whenever boredom strikes. But when a child asks the world's second most despicable question, "What can I do?" (the world's first is "What's for dinner?"), all suggestions short of flying to Hollywood for lunch with Sylvester Stallone are rejected out of hand.

Boredom is a disease that resists curing, or so I have learned, having tried to be the "good mother" who offers to drop everything to make cookies, read stories, redecorate the doll house or give a tea party for the entire neighborhood.

Now, after years of trial and error, I have come to the conclusion that the good mother is the bad mother who looks her child straight in the eye after being asked, "What can I do?" and says helplessly, "I have absolutely no idea."

There are two immediate benefits to this helpless, heartless approach. First, all hopes that you are going to rush to the toy store and buy a TV tennis game, an air-hockey board or a minibike are dashed immediately. Second, with boredom bounced right back into the child's court, the child is forced to find a way out of the situation with whatever tools and materials are available around the house. It is the something-out-of-nothing approach, which all great artists must learn to employ.

In this house we have large supplies of crayons, paint, blank paper, glue and scissors. One chest in the living room holds a half-dozen games, some cards and—what's this suitcase handle doing here? I have been too busy to reattach it to the suitcase.

Parents are chronically "too busy" when a child is bored. But out of the corner of my eye I have observed that my children often profit from it. My unwillingness to entertain them, or to buy out the entire line of Fisher-Price has forced them to think up cheap, creative alternatives to their boredom. And while some of these alternatives have had to be banned for safety or health reasons (cooking popcorn over an open fire in the living room, for example) boredom has become fertile soil that has enabled them to grow. I pass on some of their inventions—with a certain amount of pride.

1. Shoot the Shoots: The hall stairs are used as a toboggan run, with a nylon sleeping bag as the toboggan, into which three smallish children can easily squeeze and slide rapidly to the bottom of the stairs.

2. Socker: The object of this game is to pitch your sock pairs into an open bureau drawer from some other place in the bedroom. The game can go on for hours, which somewhat compensates for how long it takes to match up the socks that come undone during the game. (I have tried to induce my children to play "Match that Sock" but my children are not stupid. They know a con when they see it.)

3. Walk the Hose: The object is to walk on top of a loosely coiled garden hose without falling off. There are no prizes, although the loser has to put the hose away.

4. Making a list of everybody you want to invite to your next birthday party. This is very popular among little girls, who also like to review their class list and decide who likes them best and vice versa.

5. Making a list of everybody you don't want to invite to your next birthday. This is also popular among little girls, who can spend hours reviewing old slights and—with one pencil mark—can obliterate the little girl, or girls, responsible.

6. Making Up a New Board Game: A piece of stiff cardboard, several dozen pieces of paper, a pencil and two markers are all you need. Draw up your own obstacle course on the board; use the paper for writing different directions (go back two, advance three); and start off. The rules, beyond those mentioned, are still unrefined.

7. Playing Office: This is a terrible game, I suppose, fostering all the wrong stereotypes, but my younger son and my daughter are crazy about it. It consists of setting up two desks next to each other. The "man" gives orders to be typed, the "secretary" types them, hands them back and reminds her boss that he is having lunch with the president, jogging and going home for supper. Around this house, we play office all the time.

This is only a partial list, of course, and it would be wrong to imply that our house has completely done away with boredom or the question "What can I do?" But my children are less apt to assume that at the first sigh of ennui I will pack everyone off to the local bowling alley. Sometimes I do just that. There are only so many ways to twist a pipe cleaner, so many tunes you can play on the radiator with a stick. This is not "Little House on the Prairie." Benevolent deprivation has its limits. I try to sense when those limits have been reached.

There have been times, however, when in my inexperience I have deprived my children inadvertently. When my oldest child was four years old and his unspent energy was filling up every corner of the house during a rainstorm, I telephoned my pediatrician. It had been raining for five straight days, and I needed advice on how to handle the situation. My pediatrician was one of those rare human beings in the pediatric world who gave equal time for consultations on spinal meningitis and how to jazz up Jell-O so your child would eat it.

"He's so bored," I complained.

"Take him outside," she replied.

"But it's raining," I replied.

"What's wrong with rain? He won't melt."

I had forgotten, in my removed adulthood, that rain was fun. I hung up, put raincoats on both of us, and we went outside to slosh in the biggest puddles we could find. We made boats out of tinfoil and watched them rush down the gutters, sat down in the gutter curbs and let the water push up against our backs. My four-year-old giggled hysterically as the water rushed in split tributaries around him. Instead of cursing the rain, we embraced it. Nobody melted and we had temporarily poured boredom down the drain.

Since then, all my children have embraced the rain. In the spring they are allowed one "mud day" when they put on their oldest clothes and wallow like pigs in the largest mudholes on the playground. They return home looking like coal miners caught in a slide.

Of course, this still leaves all the other rainy days to be dealt with, endless bleak stretches of time when boredom is still the monster who must be slain. Last week my daughter gave our cocker spaniel a birthday, complete with presents, favors and eight guests, all of whom got down on their "paws" and played "101 Dalmatians," a game that seemed to have no rules, no object and no prizes except enjoyment. A good time was had by everybody. I went upstairs, cleaned my room and read a book.

THE
EMBARRASSMENT
FACTOR

One of the facts of childhood which adults sometimes forget is how circumscribed children are by the word "don't." I've never actually counted up how many times that negative creeps into my conversation with my own children, but I probably use roughly two packs of "don'ts" a day—and I don't plan on cutting down. Children rapidly slide into bestiality if there aren't any limits put upon their lives. Yet recently it is not just I who am putting limits upon their behavior, but my children who are putting limits upon mine.

Suddenly there is very little I am allowed to do. My children, who used to be such elastic, madcap little creatures, are giving me all sorts of instructions about how I should behave. The reason, and I quote all my children here, is very simple: "You might embarrass me." The embarrassment factor, like the generation gap, is an old problem, extending back through generations of children who thought their parents were all right until suddenly they were all wrong.

My own mother, as I remember, went through a period

of being a perfect example of imperfection—the more so because it seemed to me that everybody else I knew had mothers who were either flawless or, if there was something wrong with them, had the decency to stay behind closed doors. Not my mother. She was oblivious to my criticism and walked around the streets without making any attempt at all to shape up. For years she was embarrassing to me in the extreme.

She would not, for instance, wear saddle shoes and nylon stockings, like Sally Rytand's mother, who in all important ways was the cutting edge of style. Sally Rytand's mother also cut the crusts off Sally's sandwiches, something else my mother refused to do. The way she chewed her food annoyed me; the way she answered the phone seemed too enthusiastic to my ears. In fact, her very presence by my side downtown embarrassed me, since it only proved that I wasn't old enough to be downtown by myself—which was embarrassing in and of itself.

Well, the shoe is on the other foot now. Suddenly I am the focus of a rehabilitation program. The thought that I might execute a small buck-and-wing across the living room or break into spontaneous song over the kitchen sink keeps my children in a constant state of dread. Spontaneity is against the law. Eccentricities of any kind are forbidden. And that is not all.

I cannot walk up to the park and call my older son off the baseball diamond for supper. Mothers don't hang around baseball diamonds, even briefly. I cannot go to the local community center to check up on which juvenile delinquents might be influencing him around the air-hockey board in the game room. The presence of a mother in a game room would suck all oxygen from the air. And while I am still allowed to snatch kisses from my children before they go off to school, I must snatch those kisses on the private side of the front door. There must be no public displays of affection, no outbursts of love or attention-drawing endearments of any kind. My role, if I understand it correctly, is to sit quietly in the bleachers that run parallel to my children's lives and watch them draw attention to themselves.

Children have terribly fragile images. They crave attention; indeed, it is terribly important that they receive it. But while they may have fantasies of tap-dancing before roaring crowds or playing tennis on center court at Wimbledon, in a fantasy they can orchestrate things and have attention go the right way.

In real life, attention can backfire. What is more, sometimes parents can behave in ways that make their children (who have spent all day trying not to make a mistake) look terrible by association. I understand all this and try to make sure that my own behavior in their presence is dignified. But it is difficult to turn into Mount Rushmore overnight.

Driving home from school with the regular car pool in back, I turned the conversation to the subject of new clothes. As part of the list of things to buy, I mentioned that "underwear" was needed. Three bodies stiffened in the back seat. The air was heavy with inexpressible embarrassment. In fact, mea culpa, I didn't even realize until the other children had been dropped off exactly how I had erred. My children set me straight, in excoriating terms.

The cross that all children must bear is having parents who aren't even conscious of embarrassing them in the first place. "Underwear" has been scratched from my vocabulary list outside the precincts of the laundry room. But I'm not sure of my ability to keep from mentioning something much worse—whatever "worse" is. And that is my cross—to be so unsure, to not know what I've done that is wrong until it is too late to erase the mistake from the blackboard. It is enough to shake my own self-confidence, which it is imperative to retain, since a parent's job is to make sure that their children steadily build up reserves of their own. I expect, however, that we'll muddle through.

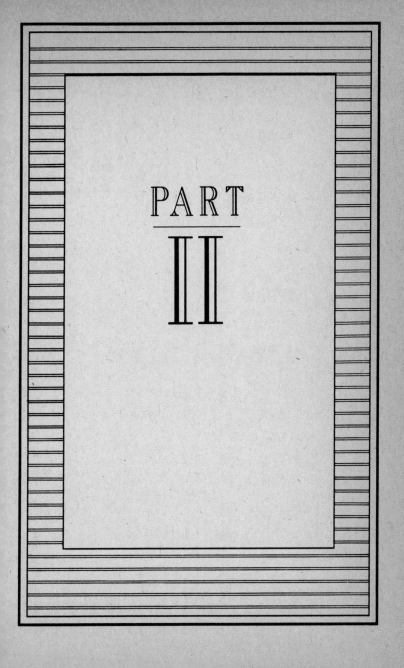

PART
II

LOST LESSONS

The other day my younger son and I had a talk about responsibility. He had lost his summer-school homework assignment somewhere along his newspaper route. I told him he had to go back and find it. He said he would not. I said that if he did not finish his homework he would have to go to bed early. He then said that school was dumb and proceeded—with lots of fists in the air and thrashing around on the sofa cushions—to denounce the entire structure of society as he knew it.

This is the usual dialogue that takes place around our house when backsliding is in progress. I took a different tack, which was to change the subject. Picking up the inside section of the afternoon paper, I read his horoscope out loud.

"Look what it says here," I reported brightly. "Tomorrow your aspirations are fulfilled, if you realize that the sky's the limit."

My son did not know what "aspirations" meant. "That means," I explained, "that what you hope will happen happens."

"You mean," he said, "like finding my homework and reading a book for a report?"

"If that's what you're hoping for."

"Well, I'm not!" he retorted. "I'd rather not go to school at all."

"Well," I said, "if you had done a little better this spring,

[61]

you wouldn't have to go to summer school now. It's all part of being responsible."

This was, from every point of view including mine, a hateful conversation, and no sooner had the word "responsible" issued from my didactic lips than he went angrily upstairs to bed—to sleep the sleep of the spoiled, the coddled, the beloved youngest child whose charm has always melted my firmest resolve.

Downstairs, I picked up Emerson. "God doth not make his work manifest through cowards." I always try to read Emerson in crucial moments to forestall any leaps off second-story decks in despair.

Fifteen minutes later there was a knock on the door. A head poked around the corner. "I found my homework assignment for the book report in my jeans," he said.

I smiled as inoffensively as I could and took him on my lap. (Is life always squaring up to write a book report on a book one hasn't read?) "Wonderful," I said. "Do you want any help?"

"Uh uh," he answered, and he then proceeded to whip through a fifteen-page book with twelve full-page illustrations about a dog and a bone—not exactly *Ivanhoe*, but it was, technically, a book. Then, sliding off my lap, he polished off three sentences for his report on a piece of paper and settled in for a little philosophical chat.

"You know," I said, "growing up is sort of like a ladder; the more responsibility you take, the more freedom you have—but each rung you climb has to include both of these things."

This was pretty abstract stuff for a ten-year-old to absorb. I told him an illustrative story about my going away to college when I was eighteen and realizing, as I walked down Fifth Avenue in New York, that I could do anything I wanted: eat four banana splits, throw a rock through a window, anything. My parents couldn't stop me because they were three thousand miles away.

"But you know what?" I said. "I didn't do any of those things, even though I was free to do them."

My son thought briefly about this. "Yeah," he conceded, "but you're a girl."

"It's all the same," I said. "Everybody has to climb the same ladder."

"I think my ladder is broken," he sighed.

"But think how much time you waste fighting off doing what you're supposed to do. Think how much extra time you'd have to look around at things if you didn't spend so much energy and time avoiding what you had to do before you were free to do what you wanted."

"Yeah," he said, his imagination beginning to take fire. "Like looking into the mirror to see how my eyes dilate."

"Right," I agreed. "Or just lying on your stomach peering into the grass. You can see all these incredible bugs, for instance, no bigger than freckles, but so beautifully designed and marked. Sometimes I feel just like God, or at least the only person who will ever fully appreciate that bug in its entire life."

"You shouldn't ever pretend you're God," warned my son. "He might get mad."

I agreed with him. My son is a natural biblical source, although he doesn't know the tree of knowledge from a copper beech.

"Hey," he said, his mind jogged anew. "Who made God? That's always been one of my questions."

A thick rope of theological study wound up as a single hair pushed quickly through the eye of a needle. "Nobody," I answered, "or God wouldn't be God."

"That's right," he agreed, dropping the subject. "But here's another question. Where does space end?"

I never went to school for that one. I told him that I did not know but I guessed that space didn't end, exactly.

"That's probably the answer," he said, "because if space had an ending then something else would have to start where it stops."

My mind was beginning to get stretch marks. I told him it was past ten o'clock and he ought to go to bed. Lying on his pillow as bright-eyed as a junior philosopher playing with the Square of Contradiction, he smiled contentedly.

"I'm glad I did my book report," he acknowledged.

"I think you made some steps in repairing your ladder," I replied.

"Anyway," he continued, "tomorrow is my lucky day."

"It is?" I queried. "Why?"

"Because of my horoscope. Remember? 'The sky's the limit.' " And with that he shoved two fingers into the air with a V for victory and was off to sleep.

Later that evening I poked my head through his door for a final bed check. He lay curled on one side, his V-for-victory arm thrust out over his pillow into space, as if reaching for something he would grasp the next day.

Someday, I knew, there would come a time when his questions would be too hard for me to answer. Someday I would not be metaphysician or scientist enough to satisfy his mind. But despite my own unanswered questions about life, looking at that perfectly chiseled, trusting face was an education in itself.

"Bethink you," wrote Sir Charles Sherrington, the famous mentor of cosmologist Sir John Eccles, "that perhaps in knowing me you do but know . . . the tool of a Hand too large for your sight as now to compass."

"Try then," he wrote, "to teach your sight to grow."

TWENTIETH CENTURY JACKS

~~~~~~

One evening my then twelve-year-old daughter challenged me to a game of jacks. She had been playing jacks for about six months and had never asked me to play with her—which was all right with me. I burned out as a jacks player about thirty years ago, although I was unbeatable in my prime.

Even Helen Sills—a prissy, lynx-eyed little girl whose sweater cuffs never hung down over her knuckles and who always carefully removed her seventeen-jewel Bulova watch before she settled down on the floor—could never get beyond "Cherries in the Basket" before I was sailing ahead with "Flying Dutchman." Jacks-playing was one of my small triumphs back in the days when large triumphs were always on another field.

"I warn you," I said, easing down into the classic side-saddle position on the kitchen floor, "I'm pretty good."

My daughter, who had heard me say the same thing at the roller-skating rink the month before, smiled tolerantly. "Sure, Mom," she said. "I'll start."

"Okay," I agreed, as she prepared to "pinkie" for the honor of throwing first. Large spirits don't quibble.

She flipped the jacks from her palms onto the backs of both hands. All but two hit the floor.

"My turn," I said cheerfully, reaching for the jacks.

"No, it's not," she said emphatically. "I get to pinkie over again."

We argued over this. The rules, said my daughter, had changed. The rules, I countered, were inflexible. Yes, no, the jacks generation gap widened with each retort, and before the game foundered on technicalities I decided to concede.

"Okay, have it your way, but I think it's ridiculous."

She threw her first hand. I leaned over to study the configuration of jacks on the floor.

"Trash," announced my daughter.

"Trash? What are you talking about?"

"I don't like this hand. I'm trashing it. You're allowed."

It turned out that in this revised and slovenly game of jacks as played by today's twelve-year-old girls, almost everything is allowed.

"Haystacks!" she proclaimed at one point, picking up two jacks on top of each other and placing them down in a more convenient location. "Mother's Helper," she said when she caught the ball against her chest. "Kissies," "Pop-jack"— there were so many ways to keep from forfeiting one's hand that the old days of "if anything trembles, you're out" were obviously gone for good.

"When I was playing jacks," I said self-righteously, "we didn't have 'Haystacks,' 'Trash' and 'Mother's Helper.' It's just like cheating, only you make up other names for it."

"This is the twentieth century, Moth—urr," answered my daughter. But finally she made a mistake that the twentieth century had not invented a "cover" for, and the jacks were mine to toss.

"I'm going to play the old, difficult way," I announced. My daughter sighed. Her mother was a masochist who didn't know how to have a normal good time.

I pinkied without dropping a single jack. (I had not lost my touch.) "Twosies," "threesies"—swiping my way through the first round of ten, I remembered why I had lost interest in the game. It was a little boring. But as I relentlessly mopped up the linoleum with my wonderfulness, my daughter lapsed into a deep, respectful silence. Then the telephone rang. It was for her.

"I'm playing jacks with my mother," she said. A short silence ensued. "No," she sighed, "she's ex-cellent." Her magnanimity made me feel small. Having "trashed" her prospects, I wondered whether I ought to hold my fire a little and fake a mistake to give the jacks back to her. But I was too hot to retire. She hung up the phone and came back to watch me play.

"Guess what," she finally interrupted softly.

"What?" I asked, as I pinkied into the fourth game. (Was there no stopping me?)

"On the math test Miss Gay gave last Friday, I was the only one in the class who got one hundred percent."

"Really?" I exclaimed. My heart twitched at the timing of this announcement. "The only one?"

"Uh huh," she said. "And if I had missed even one an- swer, my score would have gone down to eighty."

"That's really excellent," I said, purposely misthrowing the ball so that it came down on a jack.

"Ah," I exclaimed with mock chagrin. "I missed. It's your turn now."

"No, it isn't," replied my daughter, her face solemn with integrity. "That's called 'Pop-hand.' You get to take it over."

Something inside trembled. But this was the twentieth century. I was forced to play on.

ANIMAL LOVE

Over the years, this family has had enough pets to make us feel as all-American as the next family. This is not to say that any of the pets have been successful. I have a theory about this. Animals, particularly dogs, pick up whatever human instability is in the air and become its primary "host carrier." And since I have always acquired a new pet to calm things down, the various rabbits, gerbils, mice, singing canaries and dogs have absorbed the tension and gone crazy— if they weren't already crazy when they arrived.

It should be mentioned that very rarely has any animal ever been actively recruited into the household. They tend to arrive in the wake of the child they follow home or, in the instance of our present "almost Labrador," Lodi, through a child whose mother put her foot down and said "Absolutely no" when she tried to bring it home to their house. I figure that one shouldn't look for animals any more than one should look for trouble, but if it arrives on your doorstep, then you should deal with it.

Lodi was, *mirabile dictu*, never any trouble. She didn't stray, she housebroke herself almost immediately, and continues to love us with a rapturous love that overlooks all our faults and frailties. And while she was only admitted into the family on a trial basis, she won our hearts overnight. By the next morning there was no question that this small, adoring puppy was here to stay.

All went well for about a year. Then Lodi got pregnant—a mistake that happened when I was out of town and the baby sitter couldn't keep the front door closed. When I returned home, her "heat" was still in progress, and there was no hour of the day or night when there wasn't at least one male dog—usually a punkish, lustful little runt who had no shame at all—waiting to be gratified, should Lodi escape into his clutches. Retrieving the morning newspaper from the walk involved flailing a stick in every direction. Suitors lined up like depositors before the door of a bank that had failed.

I only prayed that Lodi had met up with an aristocrat instead of a bum. But mostly I did not think about Lodi's condition at all. If she was pregnant, we would know it eventually. But long before I had prepared for a nativity scene, all of Lodi's puppies arrived.

I was awakened from an after-supper nap by the sound of incessant licking. I woke up and saw Lodi, wedged into our armchair across the room, paying very close attention to her hindquarters. I arose, went over to examine the situation more closely and was horrified. Wedged between Lodi's tail and the sofa arm was a newborn puppy, but something had gone seriously wrong.

For the sensitive reader, please skip to the next paragraph and know that this paragraph is simply to describe a severely malformed puppy. Its body, from the neck down, was flawless. But from the neck up, nature had gone hideously awry, giving it a cleft head, a tiny tongue that shot straight through the crown, and two lidless eyes also above its forehead. It was barely able to breathe.

I gazed in horror at this tiny, accidental gargoyle, which could not possibly live through the night, and did what most human beings instinctively do in the presence of fear and the unfamiliar. I picked the puppy up, carefully wrapped it in a dish towel and was en route to the laundry room to put it out of sight on a shelf where the children would not see it—but I was too late. First one and then all three children apprehended me in the hall.

Christian, fifteen, coped with the sight by turning white and going back upstairs. Eliza, thirteen, being of a more practical nature, said "Eew, how awful!" and retreated to the living room to console the new mother. My eleven-year-old, Justin, however, could not take his eyes off the puppy. "I feel so sorry for it," he said quietly.

"I know," I said, "but it will not live too long, and it will not suffer." Actually, I knew no such thing but I have oftentimes tried to sweeten tragedy with false lollipops where my children are concerned; human instincts are not always correct.

It was a birth watch that was both stressful and full of exultation. Each of us was afraid that there would be another deformed puppy. As they emerged in their beautiful greenish-black bags, we watched while Lodi quickly licked off their wrappers and stroked them with her rough tongue to charge the puppies with life. Only once, when the fifth puppy emerged, and we saw a white ratlike creature inside the bag, did we worry. We thought the puppy would be hairless. It was blond.

After four puppies, my older son went to bed. After six puppies, my daughter figured she had seen it all. But Justin kept watch with me for almost the entire evening, only leaving Lodi's side for one moment to get a glass of milk.

He came back weeping. "The puppy on the shelf isn't dead like you said it would be," he exclaimed with tears in his eyes. "I can hear it making noises." He threw himself into my lap. "What are we going to do?" he sobbed.

I did not know, but I went to the telephone and dialed the number of the humane society. The person at the other end of the phone advised me to take the deformed puppy back to its mother and let her care for it as best she could.

With more courage than I really had, I gently took the towel-wrapped puppy off the laundry-room shelf and deposited it on the living-room rug next to Lodi. It was as hideous-looking as I had remembered. My son gazed at it with trepidation. Only Lodi seemed unconcerned, licking it, turning it over, and treating that puppy as casually as she did the others.

"She is a good mother," I observed to my son. He was silent. The next minute he was asleep on the floor.

After my eyes became accustomed to the puppy, I lost my own revulsion. Kneeling beside Lodi and her litter, I would gently nudge the deformed puppy back into the warm center of its mother's flank whenever it strayed on wobbly legs away from the group. Perhaps, I thought, this is the way God sees all of us—without prejudice. My revulsion gave way to a sort of quiet grieving for the little creature. Its deformities seemed more and more inconsequential. For a sliver of a second I understood the kind of love it takes to love without fear.

Before going upstairs to bed, I redeposited the puppy on the laundry-room shelf, fearing that Lodi, in her inexperience, might crush it. I assumed that it would probably have died by the time the sun rose the next day. I was wrong.

Again, it was Justin who came into my bedroom and confronted me with all the fear, sorrow and anger of somebody whose own mother had assured him incorrectly. "It's not dead!" he reproached me. "It's crying like all!"

I put my arms around him and promised that if the puppy was still alive when he came home from school we would take it to the veterinarian to be "put to sleep." At 3 P.M. the puppy was alive.

Placing it in a shoe box lined with dish towels, my son

and I took it to the animal hospital. Driving there, we talked about how bad things can happen to good puppies, how I knew that it would not hurt the puppy to be "put to sleep," how we would give it a proper burial. My son nodded, but from the expression on his face I could see that compassion for the puppy was mixed with the fear that God could do something equally as bad to a human being (i.e., him) if that was what God wanted to do.

The veterinarian's assistant took the shoe box without opening the lid. "We'd like the puppy back when you are done," I said.

Waiting for the assistant to return, my son sagged into a chair, his face showing the strain of somebody who had been in a stressful situation for too long. When the assistant returned, carrying the shoe box, she whispered, "We don't usually see anything that deformed." I took the shoe box and nodded. My son did not want to carry it himself.

We walked back to our car through the parking lot. "Where shall we bury it?" I asked. I had seen a large dumpster can near a wall that would have been a tempting possibility. If I had been by myself I might have quietly dropped the shoe-box coffin inside and said a prayer while searching for my car keys to drive home.

Apparently exhausted minds think in the same fashion. "Maybe we should just put it in the garbage can over there," he said. "All right," I agreed, as if that were a brand-new idea.

Thus it was that we said goodbye in a ceremony without any ritual and drove home in the sunlight to focus upon the living. Lodi, surrounded by her eight surviving offspring, seemed glad to have us back.

Kneeling down to examine the mewling little creatures who were crawling all over their mother looking for milk spigots, my own offspring looked up at me with new and hard-won conviction on his face. "I think we should keep them all," he proclaimed.

Reader, we did not.

PARTY TIME

It was my good fortune to grow up in a family laced with eccentrics. This is not to imply that my parents swung from chandeliers or that the various aunts, uncles and cousins who formed my second circle of socialization were embarrassingly odd. But there were other relatives who dipped in and out of my family—usually without advance notice—who were of a brighter, more disturbing hue, which is why I remember them. They gave me a taste for creative packaging as far as human beings are concerned.

One uncle had an penchant for humming "The Teddy Bears' Picnic" in the guest room (which he rarely left) when visiting. A great-aunt, (although not a "blood aunt," as she was always quick to point out) was fond of riding horses through other people's flower gardens, fixing up carburators as antiques and drinking gin out of squash trophies. There were others (some too eccentric to visit) who collected old tennis shoes, played golf in tuxedos or spent periods of time working off drunk-and-disorderly charges on chain gangs. My parents, to their credit, prized them as interesting works of art.

Now I am a parent. As the person primarily in charge of my children's socialization process, I want the world for them, which is to say that I want my children to feel at home when they are far afield, to cherish and not feel threatened by people who are not cut from the same 100 percent cotton

cloth. I have found this to be one of my more difficult as-
signments, which is why I am very pro-party. A party is a
good place to find all sorts of different people. My children,
on the other hand, view most parties as ordeals to be endured.

There are two kinds of parties—those you give and those
you attend. But for children, they are the same—events to
be avoided, unless they are with their own friends, or are
being royally paid to act as maids. Yet if children are to
evolve into adults people want to know later on, parents
have to exert sustained, consistent pressure on them to attend a certain number of social gatherings every year. Or so
say I.

A party is a slightly artificial event where one learns the
rudiments of human behavior at its most admirable: speaking when spoken to, looking somebody in the eye, shaking
hands and being friendly under duress. Sometimes parties
can even be fun, but I have learned never to promise that
prospect. Rather, I classify parties as moral obligations that
one squares up to like the negotiating table at the SALT
talks in Geneva. Something good and important might take
place.

To be fair, I should tick off the reasons why children
understandably hate parties, here defined as civilized gatherings with an overwhelming number of adults. Your children (if they are like mine) assume that the guest list will
be a terrible mix of intimidating, interrogating or boring
people who will make them feel out of place.

I sympathize with my children on the subject of going to
parties, up to a point. My point, which gains little sympa-
thy from them, is that children have to learn that human
beings thrive best in society, that we need each other, that
our capacity to thrive increases as we learn to trust and com-
municate with a wide variety of people. A party is a good

place to practice these skills. Tonight's soiree can prepare the way for tomorrow's flat tire, when you might have to pass the time with the tow-truck operator who is fixing your wheel.

So much for the theory; here is how I break it down for usability. I classify parties our family is invited to according to urgency. After announcing the upcoming event, I deliver one of the following statements:

1. "I'd like you to come, but it is not mandatory."
2. "I'd like you to go . . . for my sake."
3. "I'd like you to go, and I'll be very upset if you don't."
4. "I'd like you to go, and if you don't, I'll hold it against you for the rest of your life."

Needless to say, only the last sentence guarantees a full car en route to the event.

The last time I pulled out all the stops was last Christmas when we were invited out for the traditional evening feast on the 25th. A series of parties on other nights had preceded this invitation. I did not insist upon group attendance, which meant that my younger son went to all of them, my daughter attended one, and my eldest did not even toy with the possibility. He even tried to writhe his way out of Christmas night itself.

"I ask you to go to one party a year with us," I told him. "Out of three hundred and sixty-five days, there is only one day when I make that request. Today." (It was a fairly unassailable argument.)

"Well, I'm not going," he replied.

"Fine," I answered. "You're too old to coerce. I don't have the energy to try. And furthermore, if I did, I would be so exhausted that the party would be ruined for me.

Either you go or you don't go, but spare me the arguments. And remember, if you don't go, I won't forget it."

"Blackmail!" he shouted.

"Whatever." I shrugged, leaving the room. He came.

As parties go, this one was loaded with the kind of significance that congeals the fainthearted. It was held in a large house full of handsome, gregarious people (all of whom were related to each other) and there was a daunting percentage of silk dresses and suits. (I had held firm on attendance but made no comment, knowing it would be shredded, on what my children had to wear.) Then, too, it was the night of nights, Christmas. The psychic emotional pitch of the evening could not have been higher, and into this gathering of fast jokes, friendliness and unfamiliar faces, my children were thrust. Of such scenes nightmares are made.

At the outset, my three children huddled in the den, talking with each other. Then one of the older children in the host family approached my elder son. She coaxed him effortlessly into her orbit, chatting about school, her younger brothers and—here a great stroke of brilliance—about the number of times her father had kept her brothers out of jail. This last topic broke the ice. My son was launched.

At the sit-down supper, which extended through various rooms, the teenagers were all grouped together. My children seemed to be taking part in the general conversation, although I could not lip-read my way through any of their talk.

Then, surprise of surprises, came gift distribution. My children's names were called out again and again. I smiled as their faces registered increasing incredulity. Who were these people that they would give them presents? Shyness, replaced by delight, replaced by—finally—an acceptance of their own worth, lit up their faces. Not every party takes place at Christmas, but gifts accrue when human beings risk mingling with each other, and it was tangibly true that night.

Driving home after the party was over, there were some *pro forma* complaints. "Rich kids," said my daughter. "At supper they talked about which subway system in Europe was the best."

"Yeah," said my older son. "Subways and how rotten the scuba-diving equipment was in Antigua."

"You sound like snobs," I commented. "And it's not as if you've never left your backyard. Are you discriminating against rich kids?"

"No," admitted my eldest. "They were pretty nice, actually."

"Why did they invite us?" asked my daughter. "I mean, we're not relatives or anything."

I explained, tracing the genealogy of that family's relationship to ours: my friendship with their oldest daughter in college, her being godmother to my older son, I to hers. Through that friendship, I had met her family, and we had now been intermingled for over twenty years. The party celebrated more than Christmas. It celebrated love, loyalty and a generosity that does not keep tabs.

"They even gave us presents," said my daughter.

"More than we gave them," said my older son.

"Nobody is counting," I replied. "That's just the way they are."

Of course, not all parties are so pure and unequivocally well-intentioned. Nor are all people so easy to like. But that night my children gained an inkling of why I think parties can be important. One's curiosity about people begins to outweigh one's fear of them. We understand what had previously eluded us. Vistas expand. And, so, my children, do we.

FRACTIONS
AND LIFE

~~~~~~

Many years ago I took a civil service entrance exam that contained "ringer" questions designed to weed out the people who had "Messiah complexes" or thought that J. Edgar Hoover was giving them varicose veins. These questions were easy to spot, although the one only that still sticks in my mind is, "Do you think that you are a special agent of God?"

I paused, thought about all the government benefits that hung upon my answer and wrote "No." I would like to think that under the same circumstances Mr. Hoover might have lied, too.

Then as now, I've never thought that there was anything wrong with thinking that you are a "special agent of God," providing you grant that same possibility to the person sitting next to you. In lieu of angels (and I'm not ruling them out), human beings often act as "special agents" whether they know it or not, bearing messages, extending comfort and paving each other's roads in those despairing moments when all we are capable of is seeing potholes, or worse, dead ends.

"Despair," says Talmudic scholar Adin Steinsaltz, "is one of the supreme sins because a despairing person ceases to struggle. . . . It has a feeling of completeness to it, closely connected to smugness. The despairing person makes no attempt to change himself or the world." I agree with Rabbi Steinsaltz, who later on defined the "Messiah complex" as that feeling "that your life is not complete unless you perform a mission of saving the world in a bigger or smaller sense."

How to save the world is another question, in what way, for whom, and when? With these questions still unsolved, I got on a train one afternoon with a recently published novel by a highly acclaimed writer whose insights into life I looked forward to absorbing. But my ten-year-old seatmate was looking forward to something else.

There are three children in this family, and the middle one often gets squeezed like jam between two pieces of bread that press upon her. Today we were leaving her brothers behind.

For days she had been busy pressing clothes, rounding up socks and trying not to feel superior to the boys, whom for once she was ditching. This was our first extended mother-daughter outing. I had hoped she would use the train window as a television screen so I could get myself somewhat together. But as the train pulled away from the platform she turned expectantly toward me, smoothed out the pleats of her new dress and began to talk. After several moments, I put my thumb in my book. The highly acclaimed novelist would have to wait her turn.

Often I have looked at my small, passionate daughter and thought, with chagrin, that she has largely had to raise herself. There never seemed to be time. I have never been the kind of parent who worries over mustard stains and sews Girl Scout badges on promptly. Then, too, if there are firecrackers about to go off in the attic, hurt feelings on the ground floor have to take second place. The noise of boys has frequently muffled my daughter's quieter needs.

The mother-daughter connection has sometimes worn thin, and it is usually my daughter who must remind me that it exists, the way she reminds me every morning that it is time to get up. She has suffered from my neglect. On the other hand, she is very capable, which is what all parents want their children to be.

Her eyes were full of unexpressed questions, her face a study of anticipated answers, her small body—usually flopped on a sofa reading Judy Blume novels or sitting cross-legged on her bedroom floor dissecting her best friend's personality with her second-best friend—was erect in her seat. This was, I realized, her big moment, one of the first chances she had had in her entire life to orchestrate an uninterrupted conversation with her mother. She was taking that opportunity as her right. I shoved the world I didn't know how to save to one side and listened to her.

Boys, she began. She liked them ("as friends" she hastened to add) but she didn't like them. What did I think was the right attitude to have? I volunteered a few ideas about being nice to them while keeping a slight distance. Even I thought I sounded awfully old-fashioned. But she listened intently. Perhaps my ideas weren't as priggish as I thought.

Her friends. We counted them off together. As a whole they were wonderful, but some of them hurt her feelings. We discussed why that might be. She genuinely wanted to understand what made them tick.

Parents. In case either her mother or father died, she wanted me to know she had picked out some spares from among my friends. After all, one had to provide for all eventualities. Her choices were good. I approved.

Then the conversation turned to her future, her hopes for it, what she thought she might do. Her hopes were breathtakingly pure and as I sat in my seat and listened to her talk about what she thought she was *for* Rabbi Steinsaltz's "Messiah complex" came into true focus for the first time. My daughter is capable of thinking large and small at the same time.

"I think I want to be a teacher, or at least somebody who helps people," she said.

"Those are two good things to be," I answered. "In fact, you already are those things."

"I know," she said. "Like last year when some of the class didn't understand fractions and the teacher asked me to show Daniel and Jeremy how to do them. Daniel understood it when I showed him one way but Jeremy didn't so I had to figure out a different way. Then he got it, too."

We discussed what it meant to be creative, how when one thing doesn't work you have to dig into yourself to find another, which is where the hard work comes in. All of these concepts seemed easy for her to grasp, which surprised me. Where had I been when she was tooling up her brain?

"I really am very proud of you," I said. "You're very special."

This was a new thought for her. She didn't quite know how to receive it. "People tell me that I ought to be proud of you, too," she answered, "and I never know what to say back."

"You're right," I answered. "Pride has nothing to do with anything. If you have learned how to do something, like teach fractions, for instance, you are grateful that you get the chance."

"That's right," she said, kindling to the suggestion. "Like when Justin wrecks himself on his bike and I fix him up with pillows and Band-Aids and get him to stop crying. That really makes me feel good inside myself."

And so it went, for three hours, as we swung along the railroad tracks, knitting our thoughts and lives together like old college roommates going toward a reunion. It was the best three hours I had spent in a long time. The feeling of being in service to something larger than oneself was wonderful; I was exceedingly grateful for the opportunity which the "special agent" on the next seat had handed me. It was like knowing how to do fractions. Someone else has to want to learn about them. Otherwise the person who knows about fractions is of no use at all.

THE WORRY
FACTOR

~~~~~~

It is commonly acknowledged that the organ that gives us the most pain in life is our brain—or somebody else's in close proximity. And, according to the "EST" training I have so far managed to avoid, a great many heads are badly "wired" and can electrocute us with worries that the human being is not rubberized to withstand.

Why we like to worry is another question, as is the difference between feckless and fertile worrying, which can produce ulcers or symphonies. But once, while moving half-witted with worry around the kitchen, I stopped, mentally pushed everything that I couldn't do anything about at that moment out of my head, and then, regrounded, looked around to see who was sharing that moment with me. My eyes fell upon my eleven-year-old daughter. Her eyes were full of tears.

She needed to talk. We went into the living room and sat down. She felt terrible, she said. It became clear as she explained herself, that she had a lot of worries on her mind.

For one thing, she was not very pretty. For another, she was not very smart. She was not rich, didn't have clothes as nice as everyone else's, her brother was oftentimes mean to her, and her best friend, to quote her exactly, "totally hates my guts."

There were other deprivations, deeper and therefore deserving of a curtain of privacy that I will now draw across the rods. But it was a fairly devastating list of liabilities, many of them not of her own making, and I let her spread them all out in their full horror without jumping in like some kind of Red Cross worker to tell her that her worries were only in her mind. Of course that's where they were!

Without necessarily agreeing with her on every point, I talked about people who had more than she did, and people who had less. Some rich girls are ugly. Some pretty girls are poor. I felt compelled to add that, inexplicably, some rich girls are also pretty, which is a mystery and nothing we can truly understand. But it seemed to me, I said, that one could look at the world in a couple of ways: as an imperfect place that makes us miserable or as place that is imperfect and gives us something positive to do.

"You know," I explained, "like when you see a little boy crying in the playground. You can either say, 'How awful, he is so sad,' or go up and ask him what's the matter and try to fix it up."

My daughter of the heart-shaped face didn't quite understand this friendly-carpenter approach to existence. In her mind, at that moment, she was the kid crying on the playground and her chief worry was who (or Who) would fix *her* up.

"I used to ask God to please, please give me a nice day. But it never worked, so I stopped asking."

"Maybe," I suggested (telling my heart to stop twitching), "you could turn the question around and ask God to please let you give the day something nice."

Maybe yes, but maybe no. Maybe I hadn't heard her the first time when she listed her problems, and as we walked upstairs to her bedroom she repeated them for me again. As I watched her climb into bed I observed, "You know, if all you were were your worries, you wouldn't even exist. You'd be a minus."

Hiding under the quilt that all too soon she would be forced to throw off the next morning, my daughter tried to understand this.

"You can wreck the day you're still in," I continued, "worrying about the day that hasn't even arrived."

"But you *have* to worry!" she exclaimed, and the look on her face poking over the quilt was incredulous that someone my age did not know that this was one of the first facts and obligations of life.

"You do?" I answered. "But doesn't worrying just make you more tense by the time tomorrow finally comes?"

A small but hopeful expression flickered across her features. Perhaps, she conceded, there was something to this line of thinking. She smiled, nodded her head and yawned.

"Why don't you take all your worries," I said, bending down to kiss her goodnight, "and shove them right out the window where they belong."

Then, in a final bit of dialogue that reminded me that two heads in close proximity can produce something a great deal more significant than pain, she changed the subject.

"This doesn't have anything to do with what we're talking about," she said, "but why is it that when I cry my nose gets stuffy?"

"I don't know," I answered. "Maybe there are just too many tears to fit in your eyes."

"My tears are salty."

"That's because you have salt in your body."

"Mom," she asked, "can you taste my forehead and tell me if it's salty?"

I gave it a taste and said, "No, actually it isn't."

"Oh, good!" she exclaimed, her face breaking into a wide, relieved smile. "That means I don't have cystic fibrosis."

IN PRAISE
OF TEACHERS

One of the major responsibilities of parenthood is to educate children. I was ready for the challenge, but I assumed that between a good school and a supportive home environment it would be an easy waltz. Now we are six; now we are eighteen. Slowly (with the help of a good used set of encyclopedias) my children's minds would open, like petals on a pond lily. Well, the process has turned out to be a bit more difficult, proving two things: My children are not lilies, and while they have good minds they don't always open up for the expected things.

There was a brief honeymoon period when my original preconceptions were undisturbed. For the first several years when I presided at the front door every morning handing out rain slickers, lunch boxes and kisses, my children trudged up the street without complaint toward an institution that smelled of crayon wax and eraser dust.

Then, like new equipment that eventually develops problems, they began to show signs of wear and tear that made me focus upon the school, the curriculum and the teachers who were part of their educational odyssey. Educating my children began to feel like pulling three Mack trucks through the mud.

The oldest turned out to have a learning disability, but it was not properly diagnosed until he was in high school. In the interim, he saw the insides of two public schools, a military institution, a school for "disaffected students" (he lasted two days) and one disastrous place that specialized in drawing rainbows with expensive imported chalk. I weep to think of all those days when he was forced to show up at school and feel stupid. Adults undergoing that sort of daily humiliation at a job would quit.

The middle child had her own problems, not so severe, but still worrisome. She more or less sailed through elementary school without any major crises. But when she reached high school and was suddenly thrown into hormonal imbalance, the Rise and Fall of Absolutism in Europe was frankly less interesting than the rise and fall of various rock stars who effortlessly caught her attention. Grades plummeted. Now midway through high school, she is just catching up.

As for the youngest, who thinks in large, unprocessed intuitive leaps, he tends to view homework as something to be accomplished between record bands, which is not to say that he doesn't pose intellectual questions. Chief among them is why go to school at all when the streets are bare of breakdancers and could use a little talent such as his own?

Enter the master teachers. Praise them, memorialize them, carve their names in stone. In my long, arduous effort to encourage three children to succeed in the right schools with the right equipment in their knapsacks every morning, a good teacher is the pearl of great price that parents rightly search for and, once found, want to clutch forever to their bosoms. If I were in charge of the universe, good teachers would earn far more than cabinet ministers; the latter are replaceable, the former are not.

❭❬

As all children will tell you, the best teachers are two things—funny and fair. These qualities are also embodied in the best people, I suppose, but if a teacher has these two ingredients properly mixed together, he/she can easily keep the unruliest class firmly in the palm of his/her hand. Fortunately, my children have encountered a few of these teachers along the way.

The first funny/fair teacher was my elder son's sixth-grade instructor. Ursula Cossel was his first experience with somebody inside a school building who gave him a reason to go inside. Having spent his entire educational career surrounded by sweet, hands-in-their-laps little girls who always turned in their homework on time, my son knew there were two things wrong with him: his brain and his gender. Mrs. Cossel set him straight.

On the opening day of class, she stood behind her desk and made an announcement. "I think it's only fair for you to know what my prejudices are before we begin the year. Actually, I only have one. I like boys better than girls."

This was a calculated, electrifying statement. Every boy's head in the room suddenly straightened on its stem. Who was this woman? What did this statement mean for them?

"Now," continued Mrs. Cossel, "you may not think that this is a right kind of opinion to have, particularly since the last time I checked in the mirror I was a female myself. But in my experience sixth-grade girls are picky, whiny and all sorts of things that I don't find attractive. You can, of course, prove me wrong, girls. But you ought to know in advance that I am crazy about sixth-grade boys."

Needless to say, my son was entirely in Mrs. Cossel's thrall for the duration of the school year. His grades improved; he laughed more than he had ever laughed before 3 P.M. on a school day; and, like many other ex-students, he routinely drops in on her at school if he is in the vicinity. Over the years so many ex-students of Mrs. Cossel's have dropped in to visit that the school finally made a policy that they couldn't do it anymore. As far as I can tell, the policy continues to be ignored.

What draws them back is the memory of her candor and caring. "You had better pay attention in class," she warned them. "Sixth grade is the last stop for gas before the belt-way"—which meant junior high.

No dummy about gender development, she banned sleeveless blouses for girls ("boys can see more than you want them to") and thrilled the boys by insisting that they all go out and buy Mennen Speed Sticks to control their perspiration problems. Most of the boys didn't know they were old enough to have the problem. It was reassuring news.

Consistently her class scores higher than almost any other sixth grade in the city on achievement tests. I credit her with keeping my elder son in school today.

Entirely different, but equally as effective, was my daughter's eighth-grade teacher, Sister Barbara. A large and graceful woman who played a mean game of basketball and never missed an episode of "Hill Street Blues," Sister Barbara was the General Eisenhower of schoolteachers—businesslike, committed and not particularly anxious to get to make personal friends of her students' parents. I had always counted upon winning my children's teachers over to my side, thus unbalancing their judgment in my children's favor. But Sister Barbara never responded to this "let's be best friends" approach.

Actually, I was initially prepared to call for her resignation. For the first three months, my daughter routinely went to sleep with tears in her eyes. Sister Barbara was mean. Sister Barbara was too strict. Sister Barbara found mistakes in your homework that were so small and told you to shape up your act so often that eighth grade was beginning to resemble a long, waterless March to Bataan.

After witnessing one crying session too many, I said to my daughter, "That does it! I'm going to call up that school and ask who this Sister Barbara is. She's ruining your life."

The mere thought galvanized my daughter into action. "Oh, please don't do that, Mommy. Sister Barbara would be furious. She hates it when parents interfere." I drew back in deference to my daughter's wishes, but was prepared to attack with vehemence at a later date.

It wasn't necessary. My daughter steadied her course right after this conversation, and by the time of my first school conference with Sister Barbara I was figuratively holding a large bouquet of roses in my hand. This was the first teacher in my daughter's life who had given her the sense that she could be a real scholar. She was willingly studying in her room for hours at a time after school.

The conference itself was vintage Sister Barbara. Gazing at me with clear brown eyes, my daughter's work spread out before her in a prearranged pattern, she launched into a detailed, understanding critique of Eliza's strengths and weaknesses with specific recommendations for the situation at hand. It was rather like being presented with a careful analysis of a major corporation. I would pay serious money to have Sister Barbara come in and straighten out my own life.

There were other fringe benefits to being in Sister Barbara's class. On weekends she took the class to basketball games; arranged girls' sleepovers complete with rented movies and popcorn; and held dances. Every other class was dying to reach the eighth grade. Like all master teachers, Sister Barbara put me into a state of awe.

Consider how difficult it must be to face a roomful of

children, half of them drawing on their sneakers, and try to teach them *The Iliad*. Think what magic one must need to convey facts about the molecule to thirty students with thirty different blood-sugar levels. It is a wonder that there are still new teachers training for the ordeal.

There are, however, times when even the most seasoned and dedicated of teachers is at a loss for practical wisdom— which reminds me of a telephone conference I had with the head of my younger son's school this year.

It has been a zigzaggy year for my youngest child, who is still trying to decide whether he will be a student. Mixed up in the equation is his own low opinion of his gray matter, although he stands alone in thinking that he does not have the equipment it takes to pass muster in class.

"Sometimes," said Mrs. Ely, "nobody knows what to do, not parents, not teachers, not anybody. But I wonder if you would mind if I did one thing."

"What?" I inquired.

"Pray for him," she answered. "I have found that it helps."

I had forgotten Emerson, who once wrote, "Prayer is the contemplation of the facts from the highest point of view." In my view, that is what the best teachers instinctively try to do.

MY FRIEND
BARTHOLOMEW

One of the good but sometimes wearing aspects of parenthood is that it keeps you humble. Not at the beginning, however. In the beginning we set off like captains of clipper ships outfitted with the latest gear and tackle to race across the ocean. Then, somewhere mid-crossing, we realize that the expedition is essentially beyond our control. That time coincides with children becoming adolescents. Adolescence is a mutinous, confusing time when everybody is trying to get off the boat.

Since my children can't desert ship, they criticize the captain. I have recently been informed that my laugh is too loud, my wardrobe too secondhand and my personality too intimidating for my children to expose to their friends. And while I like having mini-adults in the household (discussion is replacing food fights at the table), I am doubly grateful for those friends who still like me the way I am—which reminds me of Bartholomew.

I never had much reason to know Bartholomew until several months ago when we moved into a new neighborhood. Actually we only moved three blocks away, but it altered my dog-walking route and put me in closer proximity to Bartholomew's family, the O'Haras. Often after supper I would tie the dog by his leash to the O'Haras' front porch and spend a half hour chatting with Bartholomew's parents, who were usually outside.

Often Lizzie (thirteen), Bartholomew (ten) and Mary Ryan O'Hara (seven) were on the porch, too—small, silent shadows who lounged on and off their parents' laps while we adults conversed. I noticed them, but only in passing. I assumed the same from them.

Then, at the end of the summer, I took a short four-day beach vacation. The night I returned home, there was a knock at my front door. Opening it, I found Bartholomew O'Hara in cutoff jeans and bare feet.

"My parents want to know if you'd like to come over tonight and visit awhile on our porch," he announced.

It was a very straightforward invitation, but there was something odd about it. The O'Haras hardly lacked for porch companions. In fact, I tried to ration my visits since they were so vulnerable to walk-ins. But I took the request at face value and invited Bartholomew inside.

"That's a nice offer," I replied, "but since I've just gotten home tonight, perhaps your parents would come visit me this evening."

Bartholomew nodded vigorously, as if I were some kind of a genius for coming up with such a superior alternative. I went to the phone.

Judy O'Hara answered and I proposed my counterinvitation. "Sure," she agreed. "We'll come after the dishes are done. But, actually, it was Bartholomew who was dying to see you. He's been pacing the floor waiting for you to return."

"Really?" I exclaimed sotto voce into the telephone receiver.

"Really," repeated Judy O'Hara.

I hung up the receiver feeling strangely redefined.

Until that moment I had always thought of Bartholomew in terms of his most outstanding physical characteristic—his hair. Since babyhood, it has grown straight out from its roots like ash-blond filaments of a dandelion, which he rather resembled at a distance. And although his parents finally found a barber who was ruthless and cropped it back to stubble, it still had the potential for flaring up overnight and reframing his head like a battery-operated aureole. I had never known anybody with such interesting hair. Now, however, I examined his face.

"Well," I began as casually as I could, "your parents said they would come over here later. But perhaps you would like to wait for them here."

"Okay," said Bartholomew, immediately dropping into a kitchen chair. I did the same. We looked at each other across the kitchen table. Bartholomew threw the first strand of connective tissue toward me.

"I bet you didn't know that I was an artist," he offered.

"I didn't," I replied. "What's your medium?"

"Oil," he answered. "Still lifes, mostly. I give 'em away, I mean, I don't make people pay for them."

"That's pretty nice of you," I commented.

"Not really," he replied. "I only give my paintings to people I'm pretty sure will give me something back later on."

I laughed but Bartholomew was serious. As our conversation expanded over an increasing number of topics, I discovered that Bartholomew O'Hara was incapable of telling an untruth.

"I don't like people to tell me secrets," he admitted at one point. "Because if somebody is doing something wrong, I'm afraid they'll get in trouble or hurt themselves and then I feel like I have to tell."

This kind of honesty, I reflected, boded well for Bartholomew's future as an artist, and a human being. He was awash in integrity. But I worried that he might use his sharp eye on me and become disappointed at a future date.

"Do you think you might bring over some of your paintings for me to look at?" I inquired.

"Sure," he said, rising slightly from his chair. "You mean now?"

"Well," I amended, "it's a little late tonight. But perhaps tomorrow, when the light is better."

"When?" he persisted.

I picked an hour at random. "Three."

"You've got it!" confirmed Bartholomew. I sensed that I was in the presence of a person of strong convictions, easily magnetized by ideals and probably a little stubborn. I wondered as I recorded the slight upward tilt of his chin and his unwavering gaze whether he ever got in trouble in school. I wouldn't want to mess with Bartholomew unless I knew I was right.

The next afternoon, promptly at three, Bartholomew arrived with two small canvases and his little sister, Mary Ryan. This being something of a professional visit, I took the paintings immediately into the dining room and laid them out on the table for examination. They were rather good for someone ten years old.

"I like what you did with that wine bottle," I offered. "Using that bit of white to catch the reflection."

Bartholomew nodded in agreement. Getting an old art book full of museum reproductions off the shelf, I opened it up on the table. The next hour was spent critiquing the masters.

"That's trash," said Bartholomew of a seventeenth-century Dutch landscape painting. "He didn't know what he was doing with that tree."

Mary Ryan was more charitable. "But it must have taken

him a long time to paint," she said softly. Before the afternoon was over, Mary Ryan had slipped onto my lap for better viewing purposes. I had forgotten what it felt like to be in the company of children who weren't looking for excuses to leave.

That afternoon was the beginning of a ritual which continues to this day. It is now routine for Mary Ryan to ring the bell "to visit," as she explains. Lizzie, a more circumspect adolescent, sometimes comes in with an ostensible reason, like wanting to borrow back the computer game she lent my thirteen-year-old son. For a few moments in time, rumor had it that she liked my youngest. Bartholomew told him to his face.

"Oh, yeah?" responded my son, smiling. "Well, thanks, Bart, I'll take it into consideration."

Bartholomew wasn't going to let that one get by him.

"I told her I didn't know what she saw in you."

Everybody, including my son, laughed. Bartholomew had put my son, the budding Casanova, in his place.

One afternoon, Bartholomew came over and asked me a direct question. "Tell me honestly," he said, gazing at the two paintings hanging in my hallway, on loan. "Which one do you really like the best?"

"I think I like the still life with the wine bottle," I answered.

Turning away from the paintings, he thrust his hands into his pockets and said emphatically, "It's yours!"

"But Bartholomew," I protested, "I haven't given you anything back."

"Yes, you have," he countered. "You moved into the neighborhood."

There are certain moments in life when you either accept a tribute or you dishonor both the giver and the receiver. This was one of those times.

"Why, thank you, Bartholomew," I said gravely.

"Don't mention it," he said. "Now, how do you want it framed? I go all the way."

"I'll leave that to your artistic judgment," I answered.

Bartholomew nodded and took the painting off the wall. As I watched him walking down our front path with the canvas under one arm I wondered how I could have ever thought of him as only a dandelion head in cutoffs. I suppose the answer is simple. My eye lacked artistic vision. But Bartholomew had expanded my vision and I was grateful, which is one way to feel in the presence of love.

ON GETTING MAD

It was dinner time. Three children sat at the table. The younger boy, six, reached for his glass of milk. Over it went.

"Don't worry," I said cheerfully. "Accidents happen."

(Actually, much larger accidents have occurred without my being perturbed. Once an entire shelf of china fell from the kitchen wall. I looked up from the newspaper and then went back to reading my horoscope.)

Sponging up the milk, I filled a fresh glass. Within moments, my son proceeded to spill his second glass of milk. "Really, Justin," I remonstrated, "pay a little more attention to what you're doing." My voice was still amiable. More mopping. Another glass of milk. But then, unbelievably, the incident repeated itself. Midway to his lips, the glass slipped between his fingers and crashed to the floor. This time I exploded.

The words I spoke are lost to me now, but my tone of voice was unmistakably angry. Shocked by his own incompetence and my reaction to it, my son burst into tears, jumped up from the table and mounted the stairs to his bedroom. Slam went his bedroom door. The next sound I heard was muffled tears.

I mopped up the third spill, went upstairs and sat down at the edge of his bed. "Listen, Justin," I said, ruffling his hair, "it's not the end of the world to spill your milk. But really, when you do it three times in five minutes—well, what's a mother to do?"

I got an answer immediately. Lifting his tear-streaked face from his pillow he sobbed, "Kiss him and tell him he's a good boy." Who could have done anything less?

I hugged him, kissed him and was so delighted at his response that whatever anger I felt entirely disappeared. But the incident only served to reinforce the conviction that my wrath was a dangerous weapon. Had I not just witnessed its effect before my eyes?

A confession, however, is in order. I am not very good at getting angry. Like a misplaced screwdriver, it is often someplace else when I need to get my hands on it. Once in hand, it tends to be a sword which I instinctively bend toward myself, asking, "What did I do to cause them to act this way?" Yet anger, properly used, is a key parental tool—unless we enjoy being perpetually backed up against the wall.

Among parents I know, there are different extremes as far as the use or abuse of anger is concerned. There is the sweetly reasonable parent who says, "Rachel Anne, I am very upset that you have thrown your dolly's dishes down the toilet—again. Plumbers are expensive. Mommy might have to go out and get a job, *downtown*, to pay for the plumber. Do you want Mommy to have to get a job *downtown?*" Poor Rachel Anne. One flush and her life with Mother was threatening to be a thing of the past. I don't approve of this approach.

At the other end of the spectrum stands my friend Liz, who once came home to find her three little boys gleefully filling in the pleats of her best living-room lampshades with peanut butter. (Actually, it was something worse than peanut butter, but never mind.) She dropped her grocery bags and screamed, "That does it! I'm packing, going home to Gramma's and never coming back again!"

My friend Liz, has yet to "go home to Gramma's," but she has a short fuse and her children routinely realize that their lives are on the line if they misbehave.

Striking a balance when we feel anger toward our children is a very difficult assignment for most parents. In this society we are afraid of anger, viewing it as a nuclear weapon which might easily destroy all life if we use it, although storing up anger guarantees exactly the sort of explosion feared. With our children we are additionally blackmailed by the knowledge that we are, technically, the stronger military power. No parent wants to be considered a bully. The knowledge of our strength can render us weak.

Originally, my view was that parents should be voices of reason, above anger, able—in the midst of the violent emotional storms that are routine with children—to demonstrate equanimity. This equanimity would provide my children with a certain ongoing sense of security. They were permitted to go crazy; after all, they were children. But I could not. I was supposed to be the equivalent of the rubber room in a mental hospital, against whose walls my children could fling themselves without getting hurt. I no longer view my role as parent in quite this way.

By attempting to maintain perpetual placidity, I unwittingly convinced my children that I could absorb anything without reacting. My infinite flexibility led them to the incorrect conclusion that I had no feelings they had to worry about at all. This is not to say that I never got mad, but it took a lot to set me off, and my children knew it. It was not in their interests to ask why.

Guilt was a great diverter of my anger. As a single parent, I worried that the lack of two adults in the household meant that I had to make up for the difference. With only half as many parents, I did a little math in my head and computed that I should take double the amount of irritation before exploding. That would make everything even—even though it did not.

Then, too, when a child thoughtlessly forgot to tell me that he was staying at a friend's house after school, or did not return home on time for supper, whatever anger I felt was so diluted with relief when I finally tracked the child down or he kicked in the front door in time for dinner that my wrath was virtually washed away.

There were various ways in which I sabotaged my own anger, while explicitly applauding it in my own children when they squared up to that emotion in themselves and let it out. I did not, however, give myself that same privilege. This gave my children the idea that my limits were limit-less—an idea which I then had to undo. It is difficult at times.

The other day, for instance, I glanced into my daughter's room and felt a switch in my head that is usually on the "off" position click "on." Her room was a mess. By the time she returned home from school that afternoon I was a towering inferno of rage, which immediately toppled onto her head.

Her messy room, I told her in graphic terms, was a direct reflection of her life and future, which would leave her no choice but to sell popcorn at the local movie house until retirement age. If she did not learn that order begins in her room, her life would never get on track.

Why I chose that particular afternoon to let out months of frustration is another story. But the look of terror on her face triggered another emotion in my head. No sooner had I shredded her with my anger than I began to feel abjectly contrite. Having "bombed Hiroshima," I wanted to follow up with massive relief aid. But my daughter was ahead of me.

"You always get mad and then apologize," she said angrily. "I don't want your apologies."

Reviewing my past outbursts, I had to admit that my daughter was right. Later on (after she had cleaned her room), I admitted to this form of child abuse and promised that the next time I got mad, I would not apologize at all.

The problem with parental anger is that it sneaks up on you. We tend, at least subconsciously, to keep lists of grievances against our children until one day the list seems too long to endure. We explode. I am learning, however, to limit the number of times I explode by keeping my list short. If one of the children skips out for the day before taking out the garbage, is rude, or commits any of the crimes that are hardly limited to children, my reaction time is quicker than it was in previous years. Out of self-preservation, I try to take exception to their behavior at the time it is taking place. This tends to keep anger of the large, unwieldy variety at bay.

There are, however, times when the best intentions are of no use. Something happens, like a dirty frying pan in the sink that shouldn't be there, followed by a rude retort, a barking dog, and perhaps a letter from the IRS inviting me to be audited. I am thrown out of control. This is not necessarily a bad thing.

The other morning, for instance, I stood like a drill sergeant in the middle of the kitchen and excoriated every child in sight for a number of offenses. Within seconds they were scurrying around to clean, polish or repair whatever they had set awry.

At one juncture my daughter started to put up an argument. (If my daughter does not go on to become a brilliant trial lawyer she will be doing herself a disservice. She is a genius at having the last word.) This particular morning, however, I halted her mid-syllable.

"I don't want to hear what you have to say. Right now, I am the one who is shouting and you are the one who is listening."

There was no logic to the above, but it was effective. Perhaps my daughter concluded silently that her mother was borderline crazy and one ought not to attempt reasoning with her at that moment. Actually, she would have been right.

My anger, although not of window-breaking intensity, was a brief but intense storm which had to run its course before the air was cleared and the dividing line on the high- way beneath was repainted, indicating on which side I stood. A half hour later, everyone had forgotten the occasion. Peace in the house redescended. Life moved forward, no harm done.

MOTHER LOVE

Her name, I was to learn later, was Mrs. Krupsaw. But when I first saw her—a tiny, wild-eyed woman flip-flopping hurriedly down the street in a pair of rubber thongs—fear had stretched her far beyond her own surname. She came to a halt where I stood with my two toddlers and their toys upon the sidewalk. "My son," she whispered hoarsely. "I've lost him. I had just left him on the porch for a minute and then . . ."

It was unbearable to be in the presence of such terror. "We'll find him," I replied quickly, the way a surgeon quickly inserts a tube into the throat of a gagging victim. Scooping up my own children, I thrust them into the backseat of my car and put Mrs. Krupsaw into the front. Pulling away from the curb, I glanced at my wristwatch. It was 3:25 P.M. At 3:25 P.M. the world was painfully full of other people's children drifting home from school.

Before we had reached the corner, I learned that Teddy Krupsaw had brown hair, brown eyes and was the only child of a broken marriage. After I turned the corner and began to accelerate, I learned that something else was very wrong as well.

"How old is he?" I asked.

"Twelve," she answered.

Instinctively, I pressed my foot upon the brake pedal. I

had not known, because I was new to the neighborhood, that Mrs. Krupsaw "lost" her child every day of her life.

That particular incident happened almost twelve years ago. Teddy Krupsaw, the helpless victim of a tidal wave of mother love, is now a grown man—more or less. He walks with a slight forward tilt to his shoulders, as if he is still hauling his mother and her anxieties behind him. More often than not, there is a frown upon his face. But my instinct to judge Mrs. Krupsaw too harshly is sideswiped by self-knowledge. I, too, suffer from a surfeit of mother love.

I don't remember when I realized that I was more than a caring parent who wanted to keep normal control over my children's lives. It did seem that I spent more time than most mothers combing the playground for my children if they did not return exactly on time. I was scrupulous about leaving phone numbers for baby sitters. A two-day trip away from home was almost not worth the effort. Something could happen; I would not be able to return home fast enough. I still wake up from daytime naps and take inventory. "Where are they?" is always my first conscious question. A part of me, the prideful part, patted myself on the back for being so conscientious. But I was to learn that mother love was more complex.

Of course, one could argue (and I did) that wanting to know upon first waking up where one's children are is simply the instinctive reaction of a mother who has dozed off while on sentry duty. Every mother wants to know that her children are safe, doesn't she? The answer I always gave myself was "Of course."

But the trick in parenting, as in life, is to make sure you are asking the right, or deeper, question. As time went on, I could not help seeing that my ability to trust my children casually was not improving along with their ability to lead more independent lives.

Other mothers, when five-thirty rolled around and their ten-year-old had not returned from the park, would think, "He's late again, damn it," and take a box of cornbread mix out of the cabinet to make muffins. I would be on my way up the hill toward the jungle gym to reclaim him or her, please God, to the safety of my bosom. Like Mrs. Krupsaw, my rib cage had fused itself so thoroughly around the hearts of my children that when I did not know exactly where they were I didn't know where I was either. Terror ensued.

It would be inaccurate to say that I had to be crouching behind the curtains of somebody else's house when my children were at a birthday party. If I knew with certainty that they were in the custody of some other responsible adult, I was not only grateful for the reprieve from my guard-dog role; I hoped my children would not be delivered back to me too soon. It was only when I knew that my children were my responsibility, that if anything happened to them I would be accused by them and by society of having been neglectful, that fear skewed my judgment.

Should a seven-year-old be allowed to walk to the local market, a ten-year-old to ride her bike across a major intersection to a friend's house, a twelve-year-old to take a bus (with no transfers) downtown? Almost always I said no, or if I said yes, I would then wait with apprehension for the return of the child in question to reassure me.

In the early days of mothering, when physical safety was my greatest concern, my anxieties were acceptable. No other woman thought I was as neurotic as Mrs. Krupsaw, for example. But other mothers seemed more secure than I was, and I envied their detachment. I could not bear to leave my children to chance.

A distinction should be made between reasonable and unreasonable risks. The world is full of awful people and possibilities for parents to worry about, and you do not need me to tell you to keep your eyes riveted upon your children when you are at the beach. But where there is a surfeit of mother love, we lose our ability to distinguish between reasonable and unreasonable risks. Everything seems too chancy. We do not dare to relinquish our control. Yet mother love, if it is to remain a healthy support for the child and not turn into a strangling vine, has to admit more and more chance into the equation each year. Otherwise our children will not pass successfully into adulthood. And if we are to pass into a more profound, solid state of adulthood ourselves, we have no choice.

I live in a city that seems particularly full of men whose hearts are fused to their professions. They are sometimes called "workaholics," for beneath whatever surface claims these men (and sometimes women) make about saving the world or providing a good living for their families, they are incapable of separating themselves from their jobs.

The woman with too much mother love is also incapable of separating herself from her job. She winds up being pulled around by her children—an unnatural postpartum condition. She either doesn't want to or does not know how to let go.

I have come to believe that the fear of abandonment by our children is partially responsible for an excess of mother love. Children justify our existence, define our limits, sharpen our responsibilities, reward us with their progress. Without them, who are we? That was the question I did not have the wit or courage to ask for a long time.

If children are like jobs, to lose them is to feel unemployed. I am not simply referring to physical loss. How many times have I caught myself attempting to please, placate and make myself popular with one of my children? Hardly a week goes by when I do not find myself rushing, like an upstairs maid scurrying to provide fresh linen for the guest room, to make my children smile.

Finally, there is the element of guilt, which can turn mother love into a monster. For the divorced parent, in particular, it is insidiously easy to convert guilt into over-protectiveness. We will pay for our past imperfect by being pluperfect in the present. Our perfection will keep our children from harm.

Thinking about mother love reminds me of my grandmother. She was a very possessive woman, so much so that when my father turned eighteen, he took a job as a deckhand on a steamer bound for the Orient just to get away from her. But one day while carrying a slop bucket down the deck he heard the ship-to-shore operator saying, "He's fine, Mrs. Grissim. I can see him now."

Not to be thwarted by the trackless Pacific Ocean, my grandmother had located a ham radio operator in her hometown and would bring him sandwiches every afternoon in exchange for his contacting the ship's radio operator. There was no escaping my grandmother after all.

I do not want to be like my grandmother, although my difficulties in reclaiming my mind, heart and entrails from those of my children cause me to wonder whether mine is a genetic problem. Then, too, if a child's heart is broken do we not always suffer sympathetic cracks in our own? Yes. But I am increasingly more aware that my children and their lives are larger than my capacity to control them. Children are born entirely under our control, but have to be released if they are to become independent human beings themselves.

How to release them is another story, which is still being written in this family. I have learned, at least partially, to discipline my wild Irish rose of an imagination without always losing my capacity to make good judgments. I am learning slowly to recognize that my children are not attached to me but to life. Yet not long ago my thirteen-year-old son gazed thoughtfully at me and observed, "Has it ever seemed weird to you that I used to be a part of you and now I'm separate and we talk to each other?"

Actually, it had occurred to me, at least the part about him being part of me. "Yes, it has," I answered, chucking him under the chin. "You not only talk to me, but sometimes you talk back." My son thought that was terribly funny and he let out a deep chortle. The cosmic miracle of talking back to one's own mother had never occurred to him before.

THE BEST THINGS
IN LIFE

When I had the cash to pursue the fantasy, I used to pore over the real-estate section of our local newspaper searching for cheap parcels of country property to buy, retreat to in my old age, and then bequeath to my children, who could live like blue-collar Kennedys in a rural compound after I was gone. I pictured them chopping wood, growing zinnias, and hanging hams in smokehouses, financially free of woe.

Unfortunately, in order to avert financial woe in the present tense, that fantasy trickled away when I wasn't looking. Utility bills, tuition expenses, and other necessities of ongoing family life had to be paid for first. Thus my dream of leaving a bucolic series of farmettes to my children has been replaced with the hope that what I can offer them now will enable them to care for themselves later.

I am aware, however, that not a day goes by that I do not add or subtract from another kind of inheritance that each of my children will receive—by virtue or fault of my existence. And while I would still like to leave them with a physical nest egg against future winds of insecurity, I know with certainty that I will leave them with something, even if I leave them nothing at all.

When my father died, he left us with his bills paid, the satisfaction and comfort of our having been there with him during his final days, and as many individual legacies of himself as he had children. Because of my father, I have a sense of the absurd (he preferred reading me James Thurber fables to fairy tales when I was little), a predilection for expensively dressed men (he always looked richer than he was), and the conviction that no problem is too tough to solve if you turn it over enough times and at enough odd angles in your mind.

On the negative side, my father did not tolerate arguments well. The practice I could have gotten standing up for myself against a strong male figure was thwarted by a man who did not necessarily believe that father always knew best but believed in the myth being perpetuated. If we were to avoid his anger, which could be deadly, it behooved us to believe it, too. Thus my father, like most parents, handed down a series of mixed blessings, and his children are still sorting through them to determine how they have affected their lives.

It behooves me, now a parent, to contemplate and plan for what my own children will inherit. Nor is this a matter of simply looking into the future; they have already received a goodly portion of what I do or do not have to give. But if, in the long run, the silver candlesticks and cash run out before I do, certain immutable, rustproof offerings can remain.

Being of sound mind and body at this moment, I would like to leave my children with an appreciation of time itself. Not the whole nine yards of it, but the small individual parcels of the bolt that unfold now and then to confirm the rest. Several years ago, when our dog had puppies, I loaded my two younger children and the entire litter into the back seat of the car and took them to a nearby field to let them romp around. The sky was blue, the buttercups were in full cry, and the field was suddenly full of tumbling children and sleek, ecstatic puppies running after each other. I made a note to remember the moment, which for an instant brought life to the trumpet edge of triumph. May my children keep a record of their joys.

Next, I hope they will remember enough good experiences to offset the bad ones, that the times we came together will outweigh the times we flew apart. Handing down experiences to one's children is tricky. What we remember is not necessarily what they recall, and I am sure there are dozens of Christmases that I labored to turn into sugarplum delights which lie on the cutting floor of their memory. Equally, I am sure that there are times I have long forgotten that are etched ineradicably on their minds. Who knows what they are? But I expect that someday I will hear about them in detail: the time we ate at some diner in Nebraska en route to a forgotten summer-vacation spa, or the occasion when I took them water-skiing on a lake, the name of which has entirely slipped my mind.

I would devoutly like to think that my children somehow understand how wondrous life is on every level, or perhaps between every level They don't have to be told that life is unfair. Any fool knows that. But mystery, like quantum physics, takes a little extra time and energy to fathom, even on the periphery. To see how "God dwells in the details" of the markings on a beetle bug, or to make the metaphoric connection between the systolic-diastolic action of the heart and the dynamics of love—these are sights and insights I would love to pass on to my children, to help them see the world round, not flat.

In the daily journal I keep, the pages are full of conversations I have had with my children, which would give to the ignorant reader the erroneous view that this particular parent is nothing but a cornucopia of wisdom waiting to be tipped over on her children's heads. I count upon my children to set the record (full of hurled epithets, importunate remarks, and paragraphs of exasperation) straight. But while I record the conversations primarily to capture my children's thoughts at that time, I can see that a great deal of what a parent does is to give their thoughts confirmation and validity.

At a particularly rough time during my older son's adolescence, I recorded a conversation we had in the kitchen when I simply said, "I know that you feel in total darkness now, and that's confusing. But please believe me that it is only temporary. One day there will be light."

He sighed, nodded his head and said, "It couldn't be more confusing now."

"I know," I confirmed. "That's what is so awful about darkness." End of conversation. Yet in all the conversations a parent has with one's children it seems increasingly important to me to give children our assurance that we have endured their same confusions and emerged to feel the sun on our backs. I suppose, to be uncomplicated about it, I want to give my children the gift of hope.

It would be misleading to imply that my battered black journal serves to file away only cosmic verities. Just now, leafing through it at random, I encountered a conversation I overheard between my then eleven-year-old son with his ten-year-old best friend on the subject of girls:

BILLY: Why do you want a girlfriend?
JUSTIN: It's just fun to have one
BILLY *(doubtfully):* If I find the perfect girl . . . maybe!
JUSTIN: You'll find one *(starts to sing).* "Somewhere over the rainbow."
BILLY: Well, what's your idea of the perfect girl?

JUSTIN: I don't know *(exasperated)*.

BILLY *(persisting anyway):* Is she skinny, blond, blue-
eyed, and very nice?

JUSTIN: You've got her so far, plus she doesn't crack
dumb jokes.

BILLY: I want the same as you, except I don't want a
sex maniac.

JUSTIN: I want someone who enjoys it once in a while.

BILLY: Me, too.

As a final bequest, I would like to leave my children with
a sense of humor. Living with them has improved mine.

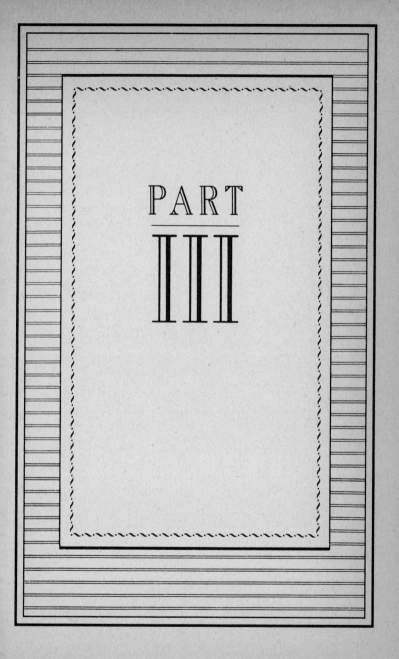

PART

III

A MATTER
OF STYLE

I grew up in a family that emphasized substance. This is not to say that we did not have a sense of style, but looking back at some of our family photographs I assess that style as conventional. The point was to conform to "good taste" or the way things were "done." That was supposed to free us to focus upon the world of ideas.

Somehow this line of thinking about style as being a quiet adjunct to the mind has not carried over in my own family. I am currently presiding over a household of roaring individuals whose minds are almost entirely preoccupied with what they're wearing, or could be wearing if only their mother was not so retrograde. Nor am I the only parent in town who is currently battling the latest issue of *Vogue*.

A friend of mine has six daughters. Between them they have shaved their heads, whitened their faces, shredded their garments and emerged from their rooms ready to contend (not blend) with society, looking like gypsy car mechanics, street sweepers, or as if they were ready to go to bed again. "The prison-guard look," said my friend dryly, "had a very long run in this household." I knew what she meant.

My own daughter of the almond-shaped eyes, swan neck and Audrey Hepburn figure was herself an advocate of the prison-guard look for several years. She never felt more attractive than when she was wearing black shoes, short gray socks, a black shirt or pants and a black sweater, usually purchased at a thrift shop. Occasionally she would wrap a red necktie low around her waist, but it was removed when she realized it might be misconstrued as a concession to a middle-class obsession with cheerfulness. I worried that her outlook matched her black clothes. Was this child suicidally depressed?

My younger son, not to be outdone in the style department, is still given to wearing oversized knickers, loud plaid shirts and a sulky Calvin Klein male-model expression. His particular fetish at the moment is his hair. Within the past year it has been natural brown, jet black, then slightly copper blond, and now is reverting to his own hair shade again. It is usually styled like an ocean in high ferment, with the help of a can of styling mousse, unknown to us in other times.

This is slightly different from his older sister's hair, which, until recently, stood almost straight out all over her head, as if she had a wet finger perpetually inserted in an electric-light socket. I have laid down the law about Mohawks. My children know that they will be invited to leave the house for good, while their mother sobs uncontrollably, if they dare to go that far.

Of course, I am hardly an example of a parent who has a firm grip on her children. Within this neighborhood are many mothers and fathers who draw the line at chewing gum in public. Four-pound earrings or hair the shape of a tidal wave are issues that never even surface in your finer homes. On those occasions when I must appear in public with my children, such as family weddings, there is invariably a terrible argument before getting into the car.

How histrionic I am capable of getting at that moment

will determine how far I can coerce them into going back to the house and altering their appearance so they don't leap forward in a crowd looking like Boy George.

I revert, usually, to guerrilla tactics. They will humiliate me, I tell them. They will look like children nobody cares about. They will make me look terrible. Do they want me to look terrible? I rarely give them time to reply. A host of political statements, ranging from "You shouldn't care what other people think about you" to "I'm proud of the way I look and don't care if other people like it," will leap like precoiled springs from their lips.

Usually their attitudes will soften if they see me sobbing, my head bent over the steering wheel. Unfortunately, I can rarely take my histrionics that far because I feel less sorrow than anger. I want to march them up to the shower and personally supervise the stripping of their heads of every ounce of plasticized styling gel that they have patiently applied. More than once I have taken a teacher aside and told her that she should not be misled by my child's appearance. The wan welfare look my children have adopted is, fortunately, artificial. They do eat three meals a day.

The style crisis came to a head last summer when my fifteen-year-old daughter had to buy some clothes for a six-week trip to Europe. Even she realized that her prison-guard wardrobe would not go very far in Crete, Paris or Florence, to name a few of the fancy stops which I had saved all year to afford. But as we got into the car to go on the shopping trip, I was already full of antagonism. I anticipated spending at least three hundred dollars to supplement her wardrobe. If that entire outlay of cash went toward new black sweaters, shirts and pants, I knew I would veer out of control.

My daughter chose to get in the backseat, probably because it was emotionally safer. I could see her dark eyes flashing with hostility in the rearview mirror. Obviously she, too, anticipated a thunderstorm. The first clouds formed almost at once.

"We can go downtown," I said, "and look in some of the places you like. But we'll wind up spending the same amount of money and getting less than we would if we went to a store I've just heard about in the suburbs."

A sigh of exasperation came from the rear. "We'll go to the 'burbs, I guess," she said sarcastically. "We always do what *you* want, no matter what I say."

I applied the brakes. "How about if we don't go shopping at all?" I hissed back. "Obviously we're going to argue the whole time and I'm not up for it."

My daughter hauled out a longer knife. "We get into arguments because we aren't compatible. I've known that for at least three years."

"Three years?" I repeated, my thoughts slightly diverted by this sally. "Really?"

"Really," confirmed my daughter. "Face it, we don't get along."

I took my foot off the brake pedal. An argument over clothes was turning into a blood bath I wanted to avoid. Glancing up at the sky which was full of storm clouds, I changed my strategy.

"What does the weather look like to you?" I asked.

"Windy," she answered tersely.

"I think we're having a windy moment in our relationship," I remarked, bringing my voice down to a more normal decibel level. There was silence from the backseat.

"Sometimes," I continued, "I feel frustrated in other parts of my life that you don't know about and it influences the way I act toward you. I'm sorry."

More silence. But when we drove into the suburban parking lot in front of the store I felt that at least one of us, the driver, had made a sincere attempt to lay down her arms. I vowed to be cheerful. If black is beautiful, then black it would be.

The entire trip took approximately two hours. To my amazement my daughter chose extremely well. While I leaned against the changing-room wall, she brought in one ensemble after another. Each was more sophisticated than I would have chosen for her, but all of them suited her well.

I was, however, astonished at one choice. The dress she loved best was straight from the land of strung lanterns and camellia corsages of the fifties: a pink-and-white cotton candy-striped, full-skirted dress that could have been plucked out of my own high-school closet. Afraid of sounding too enthusiastic, I merely nodded in agreement when she held it before me. "Nice," I said, holding my breath.

That evening she paraded before me in the new dress. Her eyes, usually shaded with kohl and looking slightly sinister, were only lightly accented with liner. The usual white makeup was gone, replaced with pink lipstick and powder. She had a strand of pearls around her neck. My daughter the semi-punk had become my daughter the demi-deb. What intricate ideological revisions had taken place in her head to effect this change were unknown to me.

Perhaps, I thought, we are not far from the day when I can take a family picture that I won't have to explain to the viewer. Perhaps we will eventually merge, blend and turn into a group of people who look once again as if we all lived in the same house.

Oddly, my children's sense of style had begun to affect my own, once referred to disparagingly by my daughter as "the Holly Hobby look" or "Style for a dead person." I am wearing padded shoulders and outsized sweaters, patronizing the same stores my children prefer, proving that youth will be observed and imitated—up to a point. I draw the line at wearing Iron Cross earrings, men's boxer shorts and men's T-shirts. But the line, I confess, is beginning to blur.

THE FACTS
OF LIFE

~~~~~~

One of the built-in handicaps of parenthood is that the world in which we were raised invariably seems like Tom Sawyer's Hannibal, Missouri, compared to the beer-bottle-strewn parking lot that our children must traverse. The assault upon a modern-day child's mind and heart from almost every quarter of life can be overwhelming. A simple bus ride home from school exposes them to advertisements for (or against) abortion, the hazards of drugs, and what to do about herpes. Which brings me to the subject of sex.

In my day—to sound like a little old lady who dries flowers in the attic—sex was rarely referred to by name. It was the aura coming from a Jane Russell movie billboard. It was what Gina Washburn did that meant she had to get married during Thanksgiving break of her freshman year in college. Today's children live in far more pornographic times.

I was determined that my own children would learn about sex the way my two older children learned they were adopted—by osmosis. Thus, when they were still young enough to be taking baths together, I would draw pictures on the side of the tub, using soap lather to make anatomical outlines. They would solemnly examine the diagrams and then go back to pouring water on each other's head.

It did seem that these shows on the side of the bathtub

lacked sticking power. The same questions (like "Where did you say babies come from again? I forgot") kept surfacing, as if last night's lecture had been washed down the drain. But I figured that teaching children about sex was not unlike teaching them how to tell time, tie their shoes or use the telephone. Repetition was the key. I would patiently redraw the diagrams on the tub and supplement my lectures with tasteful, but not saccharine, books chosen from the library. In retrospect, those were the good old days.

Then, somewhere between the ages of eight and twelve, my children seemed to lose interest in the subject. Ever the vigilant parent searching for ways to keep my horse before their cart, I looked for opportunities to continue my ongoing seminar. I wanted them to hear about sex from me, not someone else. But during the usual times when parents and children converse (around the dinner table, before going to bed, and in the car) other subjects dominated the dialogue: Who had swiped whose best friend, what "Charlie Brown" TV special was coming up, and how rotten Mrs. Turnbull's first-grade class was. I assumed that sex was on a back burner, somewhere behind the art of being "macho" and why nobody "cool" brought lunch boxes to school.

Every so often, however, my children gave me glimpses behind the curtain. They were, I realized, slightly more sophisticated than I thought. Once, my twelve-year-old daughter mocked her parochial school's idea of sex education, a topic covered in the wider "Family Life" curriculum.

"Some of the workbook questions are really stupid, Mom."

"What do you mean 'stupid'?"

"Like the question 'What is a kiss?' "

"What is the answer?"

"A kiss is a gift from God!" she replied.

Trust the Catholics to skip the middleman, I thought. We laughed and I agreed that kissing could involve a little less than God, although who would rule Him out? My daughter's school often inserted religion in surprising contexts. In her math workbook, percentages were taught with, among other tools, the Blessed Mother standing on a cloud with 10 percent signs streaming like rays from each of her fingers. (I never actually saw the illustration, but my daughter swore that it existed.)

My younger son, on the other hand, was in public school when sex education was introduced citywide into the sixth-grade curriculum. He came home after having seen a film on the subject to say that the class had been told that there was a right and wrong way to talk about "the facts of life."

"What's the wrong way?" I inquired.

"If you talk about it using baseball words, like getting to first base, strikeouts and home runs," he answered.

"And the right way?"

"You're supposed to use real names for things." He pulled out a mimeographed sheet where the male and female organs were drawn and labeled. "Like this."

"Which way did you like better?" I asked.

"Actually, I thought the wrong way was more interesting," he admitted. Again I laughed, but as time marched on, I realized that my children had been learning about sex "the wrong way" ever since they had been old enough to realize that there was something more to the subject than their parents had been willing to reveal.

My illusions were first shattered when I overheard my older son explaining to my younger son the meaning of a particularly enduring word, which rhymes with luck. I had to admit that while his explanation lacked grace and philosophical overlay, it was deadly accurate. "Where did you pick that up?" I challenged.

"Where everybody picks it up," he hurled back. "On the streets."

"On the streets!" I exclaimed. Years of bathtub lectures and carefully chosen library books had been for naught. And as I looked into my son's slightly sheepish but defiant face, I felt as outdated as a drawing of the Virgin Mary with percent signs streaming from her hands.

Of course, what children know without any parent's telling them, is that sex is pleasurable. They are sexual creatures, like their parents, and like our parents before us. But a certain modesty on both sides precludes parent and child from pursuing that aspect of the phenomenon, as if to pursue it would be to violate, on the parents' side at least, the precincts of our privacy. And while modern parents often intend to discuss this obvious fringe benefit of "the facts of life," we are usually caught short behind our own children, who have been discussing it among themselves for years.

In this house, now that there are three teenagers, the subject of sex comes up more frequently. My children do not need to know the mechanics of the sexual act; nor, I have discovered, do they need to be told that it is pleasureable. Debra Winger has already demonstrated on film what that aspect of sex has to give. Then, too, there is their own experience, which varies according to the child-person involved. How sexually involved to be is where we have something to talk about, and talk we do.

The discussions themselves must be put on the "not for public view" shelf, to protect my children's privacy. The themes, being fairly universal, can be shared. They can be reduced to several dilemmas—the difficulty of recognizing the difference between sex and love, the ability to say "No" to oneself or another person for psychic protection, and the phenomenon of guilt, which may be old-fashioned but still exists. With cause. I have defined guilt, at least to myself, as the feeling that comes over us when we are aware that something has or has not been done which we know violates our conscience. Today's children appear far more sophisticated than we were, but it is a thin shellac that covers the same questioning, trembling souls we ourselves possessed at their age.

Certain aspects of my own sexual education I have tried to correct. Having been strongly advised that it was more or less the end of the world if I was sexually active before marriage, I have stressed, particularly with my daughter, that nothing short of death is the end of the world. Sex is only part of her definition. But we talk a lot about being mature enough to handle such a large relationship, the importance of autonomy, and delayed gratification—issues that hardly stop being important once adulthood is technically achieved.

With all my children, I stumble clumsily toward perhaps the most important sexual lesson—that sex itself is one of the most powerful but most deceptive human instincts we have. A man and a woman can deeply love each other but be sexually less than perfect partners. Conversely, two people can be sexually *simpatico* to a high degree but intellectually and spiritually out of synch. Of the two couples, the former often endures longer than the latter. Like a powerful thunderstorm, sex without love becomes a memory that titillates but does not inspire. Now you see it, now you don't, although the power it exerts at the time can be immense.

These are fairly complex understandings, and it would be inaccurate to imply that I have managed to convey them across the supper table. In fact, I wonder if such understandings can be passed on academically, like the Pythagorean theorem, without the sort of personal experience that inevitably must be discovered by human beings on their own. Certainly it has not been so in my life, or anybody else's I know well enough, from which to draw conclusions. And yet, parents have to prepare the way as best we can.

I suppose the central fact of life is that there are so many facts to assimilate. No film strip or workbook assignment can hope to do the job. As for parents, I see no alternative but to be completely honest when children ask for guidance—and completely grateful when they ask. The implied compliment is that maybe, just maybe, we know something they don't. And maybe, just maybe, we do.

WHEN TROUBLE
STRIKES

~~~~~~

Not long ago, while I was sitting with a friend in her kitchen, the telephone rang; I eavesdropped on the call. The caller was a concerned mother who was asking my friend whether the boys their daughters were going to the movies with that evening were in any way capable of leading the girls astray.

"Oh, no," said my friend, who proceeded to give the concerned mother a general rundown on the boys, winding up the call with the final comment, "They both come from good families."

After she returned to the kitchen table and sat down, I said, "You know, I've come up with a new definition of what a 'good family' is."

"What?" she queried.

"A 'good family,' " I answered "is the family that doesn't automatically put the blame on you when both their children and yours are hauled into the police station for spray-painting the local school."

I spoke from experience—my own and others'. When one is raising children, there are all sorts of opportunities to meet other families, but they are not always as innocent as arranging cub scout outings or soccer league car pools. If that were so, the facades of our lives would never suffer a disturbance, our inner philosophies would never be laid on the line. But when trouble strikes and it involves more than your own child, you gain glimpses of how families really operate, how they view survival and what their notion of community actually is.

The first time I realized that there could be wide philosophical and emotional differences between families was when my older son was seven. His best friend was another seven-year-old, named Frankie. From the start, they got into a lot of trouble, hurling rocks at streetlamps, starting fires in the backyard and—the last straw—painting the backside of a neighbor's garage with a half-full can of whitewash. An irate phone call from the elderly woman across the alley whose garage door had been defaced tipped me off.

I waylaid the boys, the telltale whitewash still clinging to their fingers. Frankie reacted to my accusations by immediately vanishing down the street to his own house. Trapped, my son acknowledged that he was one of the guilty parties. I told him that after I called Frankie's mother—only a casual acquaintance—to tell her what happened, I expected both boys to apologize to our neighbor and scrub the whitewash off her garage door.

I did call Frankie's mother immediately and was entirely unprepared for what followed. She was very defensive, queried me as to how I could prove her son had even been involved in the whitewash caper, hotly rejected any idea of apologizing, and hung up the phone.

All notions of two right-thinking mothers marching their boys up to the victim's front door to speak their separate acts of contrition vanished. How, I wondered with some anger, could the responses of two reasonable adults differ so widely when they were faced with such a clearcut situation. Was this the same "good family" I observed trudging up our hill every Sunday morning en route to Mass? Did they not live in a pretty brick house with potted geraniums on the front porch? It did not add up.

There was nothing left to do but make sure that my son at least would follow through with my interpretation of the Judeo-Christian ethic as far as vandalizing property was concerned. But as I leaned against a back fence and supervised his scrubbing, I knew he was confused. Why wasn't Frankie helping? Why did he have to endure the humiliation and hard work alone?

Frankie's family dealt with the problem by ignoring the incident but sternly instructing Frankie that he could never play with my son again, which was rather like instructing water not to flow downhill. I would have welcomed the joint action of both families' informing the boys that they could not see each other until they had learned how to be responsible. Instead, my son got a slammed door in his face and the sense that he was, in Frankie's family's eyes, irretrievably bad.

Worse trouble beset another family in our neighborhood. Their oldest son, then thirteen, got heavily involved with drugs. I knew, because I was a close friend of the boy's mother, what agony and embarrassment they were enduring. But the pain was compounded by their eleven-year-old daughter's best friend, who told her that her family said she could not play with her anymore. Presumably this action was taken to make sure the contagion did not spread in any new directions but the family was served ostracism at precisely the time when casseroles and compassion were in order. I have never felt quite the affection I used to for the family who didn't want to get involved. Every time I see them, that incident rankles in my mind.

This is not to say that I am not as paranoid as the next parent over the caliber of the friends with whom my children associate. I discourage liaisons with kids who keep loaded guns in their bedrooms, smoke pot with their parents after supper or simply seem like depressing influences. For the most part, my children reject these potential candidates for friendship, too. I am not running a social-service agency or a walk-in psychiatric clinic. To assume the burdens of other troubled children is to assume, incorrectly, that my shoulders are ten miles wide.

But while parents have to act with subtle effectiveness to ensure that their children are surrounded by wholesome influences, I find it goes against the grain to ignore families when their children throw them into crisis, or worse, to make judgments against "good family" status if a child in the family falls seriously from grace.

Perhaps because we have lived in the same neighborhood for over a dozen years, I know a number of families whose children have spent a little time in reform schools or psychiatric institutes. We live in pretty houses with pretty flowers outside and the makes and models of our cars are fairly up-to-date. But not everybody is taking off for violin camp or winning trophies in "I Speak for Democracy" contests. And I seriously question how pretty a community really is when one of the families in it gets into trouble and is shunned instead of helped.

I have learned, however, not to throw my own troubles open for community inspection without exercising due caution. Your friends will understand, but that is because they see you in a larger context. Acquaintances may only have the footprints of your youngest son in fresh concrete by which to judge. Today's incomplete picture can become tomorrow's erroneous reputation which one of your children may spend years trying to live down.

Then, too, when two or more children are gathered together to make trouble, don't automatically assume that their parents will appreciate hearing about it from you. For a number of years I was a part of a small minority of parents who tried to form a steady support group to make sure that our children did not get too far out of line.

Some parents did not believe their children could ever be involved in anything even faintly larcenous; other parents thought I was seeking to dilute my own child's guilt by implicating their own; and one parent actually threatened to sue me for passing on unverified information. With more nerve than I actually felt I replied tersely, "Get in line."

I no longer seek to muster community quorums so zealously. I know which families can be depended upon to listen and which families will slam down the phone. I am no longer so interested in how or why my child got involved in pitching snowballs from the school playground at passing buses. Where once I attempted to conduct Grand Jury investigations, I now hold brief hearings in my living room and decide, based upon the evidence at hand, what the solution to the problem should be.

One dilemma continues to plague me. If I hear, through one of my children, that some other neighborhood child is seriously on the road to self-destruction (experimenting with drugs, talking about suicide, for example), I have to weigh where my responsibilities lie—to my child who has sworn me to secrecy or to the family whose own child could be in danger.

My response usually depends upon whether I know the parents. If I do, I pick up the phone and pass on what I stress may not be accurate information, for them to track down. It is what I would want another parent to do for me. On other occasions, I do nothing at all with what my children tell me. The parents involved do not, in my previous experience, want to know what they do not know.

It takes a certain gritting of the mind and teeth to ask questions of our children that will yield the wrong answers.

But most of the trouble my children have encountered, academically or socially, has been exacerbated by my reluctance to face up to reality or my disinclination to believe that all is not entirely well.

Then, too, parents suffer from failure of imagination. Who would think that two twelve-year-olds might fill a bicycle wheel full of kerosene, light it and send it rolling down the alley. Our creativity has been siphoned off years ago into other, more mundane pursuits. But when the telephone rang from the woman down the alley to report the rolling wheel of fire, I could only pray that it was a call from somebody in a "good family." Fortunately for me it was.

"Listen," said the woman on the other end of the line, "I hate to tell you this but I've just doused a burning bicycle wheel with my hose and screamed at your son and his friend for almost incinerating our garage."

I apologized profusely and told her that I would come right down.

"Don't apologize," said the unknown caller with amazing lightheartedness. "I was at your end of this kind of a call for years."

"You were?" I said.

"Yes," she explained, "until my youngest son finally retired his slingshot, I spent every waking moment wondering who would be telephoning next. I have read your son the riot act and he seems, at least temporarily, quite intimidated. But I did not tell him that I was overjoyed to be on the other side . . . at last."

Since that conversation, the unknown caller and I have become good friends.

FOREIGN LANDS
AT HOME

When I was growing up I had two families: one for every day and another for special occasions. I commuted between the two. In my house, the routine basics of life were provided: food, shelter and emotional support of an ongoing nature. But several blocks away, excitement filled the air. At my aunt and uncle's house, which served as the local headquarters for a world peace organization, I could push through their front door after school and bump into an exiled princess from Czechoslovakia, or maybe a student delegation from Korea. Thus I reached adulthood thinking that the ideal household should combine both routine and excitement or, more precisely, routine excitement. I have been expanding upon, revising, or regretting my fascination with this idea ever since.

Then I had a family of my own. When we moved into a large house with more bedrooms than children, I thought I might have a real chance to work out this idea in reality. With boarders. Financially, it would be a boon. And my children could be effortlessly educated by people from foreign lands who would tell us, over supper, about Shanghai after the Communist takeover in '49, or perhaps make music after dessert.

"Would you play us something on your violin, Itzak?" I would entreat the Jewish exchange student from Haifa, who would then fill the house with songs from *Fiddler on the Roof* as we loaded plates into the dishwasher. That was my scenario. But it was not quite the way the scenario worked out.

The first boarder was a French girl who thought she was too good for our family. Probably she was. Next was a young man from Nebraska who spent all of his time in the basement, thinking. We never saw him at all. The third woman came to us via a friend who gave me a resumé that didn't quite match up with the woman's real story. Athalie was not a cultured divorcée who needed a rest; she was a runaway inmate from a sanitarium.

Getting my "foreign lands at home" idea off the ground was difficult, and I will only know years from now whether those first boarders who floated through the house had a negative effect upon my children. At that time they were toddlers and, as a boardinghouse keeper, so was I. But certainly my children have their memories of their favorite tenants, and one of the ways we entertain ourselves around the dining-room table is to tell current boarders about their predecessors.

At the moment we are hosting a seventeen-year-old English boy who is interning at a Senator's office between his high school and university education. Robert makes quite a contrast to last December's guest, Gladys, a charming but intractable seventy-four-year-old street person who refused to take government assistance, as was her due, for an injury incurred years before when she was hit by a car.

"What ah say is what President Kennedy said: 'Ask not what your country can do for you but what you can do for your country,' " she responded when I tried to explain certain benefits she could receive.

My children reacted to Gladys, who mostly sat in our kitchen reading *National Geographic*s, in different ways. My older son was solicitous; my daughter thought Gladys extremely interesting; and my youngest felt compassion to the point of nausea. "I just can't eat at the same table when she's there, Mom," he explained, feeling embarrassed. "She makes me feel queasy."

Our house never shone more than when Gladys was living here. She could barely move, but she insisted upon polishing all our brass and silver while she sat in our kitchen. Finally I did find her permanent lodging elsewhere. But she is forever engraved in our family's mind.

In truth, there are fairly long periods when nobody but the immediate family occupies the premises. And several years ago we moved out of the large house and into a smaller one, which effectively ruled out any tenants—or so I thought. But still we seem to have lodgers, coming for the day, the week, or several months. And as the children have grown older, their tolerance and even delight in having somebody new in the house seem to have increased. My original conviction—that a thick soup is better than a thin one to nurture a family—has proved to be sound one, and a number of people have graduated from tenants into family members at large.

It would not do them justice to include Steve from Brooklyn or Sylvia from Chicago. They deserve separate books of their own. But perhaps the most memorable boarder ever to occupy a room in our house was Vivadet, a nineteen-year-old Cambodian boy who came to our house not to live, but to die.

His history, as told at our local church by the priest who

was seeking lodging for him, was stark. Only three weeks earlier he had arrived in this country (Cambodia was in the process of being ravaged by the Communist Khmer Rouge) to learn English at a Catholic university nearby. He developed a lump on his knee, was admitted to the attached Catholic hospital and was diagnosed as having bone cancer. The doctors had to amputate his right leg in order to keep the cancer from spreading.

Vivadet spoke French, in addition to his native language, but no English. Cut off from his family, with no money and no friends, he needed two things: a roof over his head and anywhere from six weeks to an indefinite number of months, during which time he would surely die.

My then husband was apprehensive. "Do you want the children to be around somebody who is dying?" he asked. Somehow, I couldn't relate to the question. But when Vivadet arrived, the family instantly related to him.

A tall, painfully thin boy with a shaved head, Vivadet came hopping into the house on a pair of crutches, his right pants leg pinned up in a roll.

"Where is your leg?" asked my seven-year-old, Christian. Vivadet giggled. He didn't know any English but he understood the question by the intensity of my son's gaze at the leg that wasn't there.

Within a week, the boy who came to die was hopping around our kitchen doing the dishes, bowing like a whooping crane to pick up stray napkins from the floor. After they came home from various schools or playgroups, the children would descend upon him like Lilliputians, wrestling him to the floor.

Continually they swiped his crutches as a joke. Vivadet would hop around the house trying to catch them, giggling as he went. Finally the children would tire of the game and say, "O.K., Vivadet, you can have them back," and Vivadet would wave them menacingly at them. Eventually he got a prosthetic wooden leg, and then the game became "Swipe Vivadet's wooden leg." But Vivadet was harder to catch once he got a new leg. Finally the children gave up.

I knew, during this time of recuperation from the amputation, that Vivadet was experiencing intense pain. He never mentioned it. After supper, he would swallow pain pills over the kitchen sink—the only indication that he was in agony. But his grin never narrowed and his courage never flagged.

Within six months he had gotten himself back in school, found a student apartment to live in and mastered almost perfect English. Then he came back to visit on weekends, beating us most of the time at Scrabble. He was a ruthless Scrabble player, laughing that high, delighted laugh whenever he scored a coup on the board. He was, his doctors knew, dying. But everything else about Vivadet was flourishing, including his hair. It was stubble length when he first came to live with us and shoulder length at the end.

Characteristically, Vivadet chose to die politely—out of the country. He asked for and received a grant to study in France. Several months after he arrived there, he checked into a hospital on the Riviera and breathed his last breath.

A large memorial service was held here at the university chapel, where I had first heard about him. The chapel was full of people, all of whom had come to know and love Vivadet for his extraordinary self. After the service, the priest invited anyone who wanted to to say a few words about what Vivadet had meant to them. Many came forward. The last to do so was my youngest son, Justin, then six.

"I feel sorry for Vivadet," he said. "When I die I want to be buried right next to him."

That wish was uttered a long time ago and he does not even remember saying it. But only a week ago, when he was sorting through some old photographs stuck in a bottom drawer of a desk, he let out a whoop.

"Vivadet!" he exclaimed, thrusting the photo toward me. And so it was—the only picture we have of him. He is sitting on our sofa, with all three children perched on his lap, opening up a Christmas present. As usual, he is grinning, as was my son now. Vivadet's tenancy has turned out to be permanent, his place in our family more than lifelong.

KEEPING
THE FAITH

~~~~~~~~~~~~~~~~~~~~~~~~~~~~~~~~~~~~~~~

Not long ago I asked my thirteen-year-old son an innocent question. In retrospect, there probably is no such thing as an innocent question, at least not when a parent is doing the asking. By the time my son had finished answering, my own innocence was in shreds.

"Tell me," I inquired one evening after supper, "where do you imagine yourself living when you're grown up?"

"New York City," he answered matter-of-factly. Obviously, that question had been settled some time ago in his mind.

Privately, I wished he had chosen a slightly more bucolic setting in which to work out his destiny. But no self-respecting thirteen-year-old gravitates toward tranquillity except when sleeping, and I, too, had dreamed of living in Manhattan (with endless nickels to spend at the Automat) when I was his age. Part one of his answer squared with self-memory. But parts two, three, and four did not.

"I'm going to live in a huge apartment," he continued, "and it will be totally modern, but totally!"

There was an emphatic tone to his words that cast a mild slur against his present environment, but I pursued his vision.

"You mean with lots of glass coffee tables and puffy leather sofas."

"Right," he confirmed. "And I'll live with a girl and two huskies, only the female husky will be spayed. Well, no, maybe I'll let her have one litter and then spay her."

I bypassed the question of living with a girl as being too complex for me to handle at that moment, and having presided over the birth of more puppy litters than I have ever known what to do with, spaying his future dog seemed reasonable to me. But there was an overall sterility to his dream that was somewhat upsetting.

"How do you plan to support yourself?" I asked, since huge New York apartments with puffy leather sofas are beyond the reach of your average meter reader.

"I'm going to be a male model," he replied.

"Oh!" I exclaimed, the way one involuntarily exclaims "Oh!" when bumping into a door.

It seemed wiser to walk around the issue of being a male model and hope, in the years I had left as a formative influence, that he might be persuaded to do something a bit more substantive on the side—like work for the Red Cross Ethiopian relief team or research organ transplants. As I silently digested my son's words, I realized I had hit a moment when having faith in him was harder than usual. Yet, increasingly, I have come to believe that beneath all the other duties and obligations that go with the vocation, having faith in your children is what parenthood is all about.

At the outset, faith in one's child springs as naturally as the love we feel for a new baby that was somehow miraculously produced by us. One does not need to have faith when one holds such a flawless, vulnerable, and utterly mysterious little creature with such perfect skin, equipment, and such trust in her eyes. No, in the beginning, we need to have faith in ourselves, our pediatrician, and the local hospital, should it be needed. Our child is without blemish—a belief that sustains us and even sharpens our wits as we cast a gimlet eye on any doctor, nurse, or baby sitter who might tamper with the goods.

Then, inevitably, comes the day of revelation in the neighborhood playground, when little Bronwyn thumps another child in the sandbox with her shovel, and without any provocation. How can this child, whose environment has been so full of lullabies and entrancing crib mobiles be so antisocial? We rush to her side, pry the shovel from her hand, and give a lesson in sandbox ethics. Where, we ask, did we go wrong?

Well, I suppose every parent goes wrong by producing other human beings who have strengths, weaknesses, and an uncanny ability to dash our plans for their character development. And that is when we need to remember how it felt to be a child.

We were blobs of passionate protoplasm, largely inarticulate, fearful of being laughed at, desperate to prove that we amounted to something, prone toward skinniness or chubbiness, shy, clumsy, terrible at fractions, bedwetters. Really, childhood could almost be compared to a long disease that finally tapers off, but not until we have prevailed over an awesome list of symptoms. Then think of having parents during this same period who may or may not believe we will ever get well.

I know adults who remember their parents as being entirely preoccupied with themselves, and rarely coming near them. Other friends of mine had mothers and fathers who silently expected excellence as a matter of course. Like tennis coaches, they winced at every ball their child hit into the net.

Well, I am not the parent of a professional child tennis player, but I identify with the syndrome. When one of my children says, "I need something to read. Hand me the *TV Guide*," a stone rolls across my heart.

Where did these barbarians come from? How, in a house with a piano and a stack of Clementi sonatinas on top, can there be such a preference for rock groups who don't even know how to sing? And does it count for nothing that the adults these children routinely meet are people who put a high premium on ideas, conversation, and extending themselves toward one another in a spirit of mutual inquiry? Apparently not.

Recently I gave a dinner party, which I hoped, at least on the periphery, my children would attend, all the better to learn what it would be like when one day they would be at the center of the action. One child stayed around long enough to get the food and then left—to watch a home movie about World War II psychopaths at a friend's house. Another child adamantly refused to come downstairs at all. And the third did engage in a brief conversation with an attending adult, primarily because he was cornered in the kitchen and couldn't think of a polite way to extricate himself.

What did I do? I ignored the first two children's behavior and lavishly praised the third for his outstanding social prowess, which I exaggerated slightly but hoped would be an incentive for him to repeat the behavior at a future gathering. It did not help, however, for me to see a twelve-year-old boy, who had come to the party with his parents, eagerly sing his favorite hymns when the focus turned toward the piano. If that had been my child singing Beethoven's "Ode to Joy" with such gusto, I think I would have asked God to take me now, while I was so deliriously happy.

Once I sighed and said, "I wonder if any of you children will ever willingly listen to a Bach cantata?"

"What's a bob cantata?" asked my daughter. I suppose I

should have praised her for her intellectual curiosity, but I fell silent instead.

It would be misleading for you to assume that this parent's expectations for her children revolve around their ability to crack jokes in Latin, play the accordion, or bring home soccer trophies. Nor am I continually monitoring their moral character . . . except when I am monitoring it. Yet the faith one needs to have in one's children is a continual exercise to see beneath their surfaces, where the real struggling, doubting, and silently self-accusatory children live. As philosopher Étienne-Henry Gilson once wrote, "Faith does not see truth clearly, but it has an eye for it, so to speak."

Sometimes your children themselves clear your vision, just when you thought that, faith or no faith, you were in charge of a downwardly mobile household where, despite the tutors, pep talks, and praise, all was going to be lost.

One day, for instance, my daughter came into my room and asked me a question.

"Can you give me three adjectives that best describe you?" she asked me.

"Oh, dear," I protested. "I'm afraid I'm too self-conscious to do that."

"I'm not," she said. "The three adjectives I'd pick to describe myself are 'ambitious,' 'liberal,' and 'jaunty'!"

The last adjective made me smile. "Jaunty," I repeated. "Well, I think that sounds just right. You are jaunty. It's one of your best points."

She smiled with self-recognition and continued. "If I had three wishes, do you know what they would be?"

"No, tell me," I replied.

"I'd wish to have a large heart, to be the most beautiful girl in the world, and to have success in whatever I set out to do."

My own heart expanded. They were such good wishes,

although I couldn't keep my mouth shut about being beautiful.

"Perhaps you might wish to be the tenth most beautiful
girl in the world. It would be an awful burden to be number one."

"You have to think big," replied my daughter, "and I'm
one of those people who do."

I put my arms around her and administered a hug of
appreciation. My "jaunty" daughter had reminded me that
a small faith is no faith at all.

THE PARENT
AS AUDIENCE

~~~~~~~~~~~~~~~~~~~~~~~~~~~~~~~~~~~~

Perhaps the earliest memory I have as a parent is looking at my children. I looked at them when they were awake and pitching about the backyard like Kewpie dolls adorably smudged with mud splatters. I looked at them when they were asleep, like faultlessly carved angels flung upon their beds. And when they nodded in my arms, warm weights against my chest, I looked at them through a tangle of shiny hair that smelled of new grass and oxygen. Parenthood is a very sensual experience but the first feast is a feast of the eyes.

My eyes also operated like those of a sheepdog on duty. I worried more or less continually that if I ever stopped taking head counts one of my children might slip soundlessly down a rabbit hole I had neglected to plug. In fact, one of my earliest joys as a parent lay in knowing that at the end of the day I had once again ushered three babies back to their beds, against the odds, unscathed and peaceful. Happiness was a houseful of safe, inert bodies. Actually, it still is.

There is, however, another kind of parental looking which is both crucial and ongoing—the parent as audience. In this role we applaud our children into existence, stroke them with our eyes toward greater feats of daring that might otherwise go undone. "Watch me!" commands the five-year-old, clinging with a death grip to the edge of the swimming pool. And we do watch him as the hypotenuse between one angle of the pool and the other is negotiated. We have borne him across the deep with our eyes.

There comes a time, however, when a parent's eyes narrow. We begin to view our children as recorders full of blank tape that we must fill up with enduring wisdom before they leave town. In this, the instructional phase of parenthood, it is the parent who implores the children to "Watch me!" If they want to catch our attention, we are equally as intent upon trying to catch theirs.

My children are just as resistant to onslaughts of adult wisdom as any other children. When I am sitting across the table from them, like an overly earnest camp counselor trying to teach them the ropes, their eyes tend to slide sideways or glaze over. They drum their fingers on the table, turn up the radio, plead fatigue. Sometimes I feel less like a parent than a term paper looking for a chance to be read.

Will one child learn about delayed gratification? Another child ever feel confident? Yet a third child understand the cause-effect relationship between honesty and peace of mind? Since the day one son brought home a nice (but not his) jacket from the playground and I marched him back up to the park to return it, I have been, like all parents, an unpaid moral theologian, social adviser, and educational counselor. I give myself a C-minus for effectiveness. And my frustration sometimes boils over into rage.

That is where, in my experience, the parent-child relationship falls apart—in the rage stage, where our children, despite our advanced technological assistance, insist upon resisting. Then a parent's eyes can flash with fire, not confirmation, and we wind up becoming a hostile audience. Breaking that hostile pattern can be difficult to do although fortunately our children can be of help.

A turning point came last year when my frustration with my teenaged daughter had mounted to an all-time high. She seemed to have a bottomless capacity for three activities: listening to rock records, talking on the telephone and leafing through back issues of *Mademoiselle*. All of these activities took place within her room, and my dilemma was how to blast her out of that room into a wider world. The assignment met with failure at every turn.

The suggestion of part-time jobs after school met with steely recalcitrance. After-school activities were rejected, along with slumber parties, trips into town, and sports programs. I believe in a little regression from life to recoup one's energy, but there was a lot of regression in this instance. Something had to be done.

One afternoon when she came home from school I announced that there was a teen club meeting at the local church that I expected her to attend that evening. "Just to see if it might interest you," I amended. "I'm not asking you to sign up for the rest of your life."

There was a wild and powerful resistance. She wouldn't know anybody. "Yes, you will," I countered. "Theresa's going." She accused me of rigging the deck, which was true. I had researched the teen club so thoroughly that I had left her no reasonable way out—and then my daughter exploded.

"You don't think I'm good enough for you!" she shouted angrily. Dropping down on the kitchen stairs, she sank her head into her hands and began to weep.

She had uttered a half-truth that landed with the force of an MX missile upon my consciousness. A great deal of love which had been circulating within my heart suddenly found an exit and flowed directly toward the thirteen-year-old on the stairs.

"Oh, no," I protested. "Don't ever think that. In fact, I think you're better than I am." And for the next forty-five minutes I sat, one arm draped around her shoulder, telling her exactly how much better she was. We wound up in an embrace.

Since then I have begun to drop back to a row deeper in the audience. I have learned to give my children more breathing space. More trusting of their instincts, I am more of a witness to their lives than I am a stage director. The benefits from this change have been immense.

Those human tape recorders I felt such an obligation to fill up have turned out to have information to feed into my own tape recorder. I am doing a lot of listening from my seat in the audience. And laughing. After supper we often have "Imitation Hour," when one or more of the children launch into finely honed caricatures of various teachers or friends. Their gift of mimicry is superb. Yet would there be an "Imitation Hour" if there was no audience to appreciate it? Probably not. Parents are crucial, but not in the way I had first thought.

This is not to say that I have chucked all my "term papers" on life and no longer search for air time in which to deliver them. But I search less anxiously and am more content to wait until asked for an opinion. Oddly, I seem to be busier in the advice business than I was in earlier days. And having ceased being such a compulsive instructor, there is more room in my life for other kinds of parenthood. Just the other morning, for instance, I found myself looking at my children again, just for fun.

It was a Sunday morning. Outside, the earth was covered with snow. My son, the dauntless paperboy, had crunched through several miles of it with a friend, who had accompanied him back to the house once the route was done. When I came downstairs around 7 A.M., both boys were sound asleep on the living-room floor.

The living room had begun to fill up with morning sunlight. It streaked through the French shutters, laid bars across the Oriental rug and touched the apricot-colored cheeks of my son, who lay limp with sleep beneath a patchwork quilt. "I must remember this," I thought, easing myself into a wing chair.

Soon, I knew, the house would be ringing with phones, plot and personality developments. The dog would remember it was hungry, the cat would scratch against the door, and in due course, the boy under the quilt would toss it off, to fill the air with new demands. But for a moment life was still and I dozed along the margins of the picture, utterly content with what I saw.

RICHER FOR
THE EXPERIENCE

One of the questions that most children carry more or less continually in the back of their minds is, "What will I be when I grow up?" This is a serious question. Whenever any of my children pose it, I try to give them lots of elbow room, hinting that there are any number of possibilities— given their talents, some of which are still undeveloped. But of one thing all three of my children are positive. Whatever they become, they will, concomitantly, be rich.

These are the same children who search under sofa cushions for soft-drink money, rake lawns for movie tickets and fix their own bicycles when broken. They have never received a stock-dividend check in the mail. But now and when are two different realities; when they grow up they plan to be surrounded by boats, ballrooms, ranches they never even visit and maids who reverentially drop their eyes whenever they sweep past.

"Well," I said, "if any of you do strike it rich, all I want is a paid-up log cabin near the ocean, for peace of mind."

"That's all you're interested in?" sighed my daughter. Peace of mind is the last thing on hers. My daughter, who was twelve when we exchanged these words, wanted thrills, spills, and a fame that would peak at the same time her favorite English rock group, which never answered her fan letters, had sunk irretrievably into oblivion. She planned to arrange an "accidental" meeting with them in a London pub and pretend, upon being introduced, that she had never heard of them. Her revenge (saturated with a generosity they don't deserve) would be sweet.

There are, however, ways in which children can "fast-forward" their lives—primarily through pretending that they have already arrived at the top of the mountain. I was reminded of this the other day when an old photograph I had snapped fell from the inside of a book. It was a bad shot, the light was poor and the two twelve-year-old girls (my daughter and her best friend, Juliane) standing self-consciously on the back porch are slightly blurred around the edges. But there was nothing blurred about the occasion that prompted the photograph. I remember it well.

That afternoon I was to drive them both, dressed in their mothers' old cocktail dresses, costume jewelry and sequinned evening purses, to a "Rich Ladies' Tea Party." This was not a spur-of-the-moment idea. The eight girls who were due to convene at a neighbor's house several minutes after I had snapped this picture had been building up to the event for months.

Each girl had a separate dossier and name to match the contents of her folder. Over dozens of schoolyard lunches, they had tried on different lives, lifestyles and number of children they would have, and had finally settled, individually, on the existence that suited each best.

My daughter's resumé was disgustingly impressive. She had chosen the name "Gwendolyn Juliette Farnsworth," wife of "Preston Langley Farnsworth." She had four children, Quincannon Eloise, Diana Lauren, Godiva Elizabeth, and Preston Langley, Jr. They had been produced, more or less effortlessly, between tennis matches and trips abroad, and none of them was any trouble, being either in boarding school (the rich woman's alternative to reform school) or married.

The object of the afternoon, as I was led to understand it, was for all these rich and indolent women to revel in their leisure, swank it up with velvet, pearls and tatty fox wraps in the Felicia Grimaldis' living room, drinking tea and talking about how fabulous the rich life was. They were, my daughter explained, all in their fifties and wealthy. "We're not rich; we're super-rich," she said.

En route to the tea party, we passed an intersection where several boys their ages were standing by a bus stop. Both girls dived, plastic pearls clanking against themselves, for the floorboards.

"Do you know them?" I asked.

"No," they answered simultaneously. Apparently if one is super-rich, it is all right to lie.

I pulled up to the Grimaldis' attached brick town house and let the girls out. As their chauffeur, I had been given instructions—drop them off and leave. Inside, various fac-simile rich ladies with names like Jacqueline Manderly Kingsbury, Genevieve ("Vivi") Chamante Charnelle, Felic-ity Grace Chamberlain and Tiffany Gloria Wallingford awaited my daughter. I marked time until the tea party was supposed to be over and then, violating my daughter's in-structions to "honk only," rang the bell and walked inside.

The site of this retrograde, capitalistic pig-out was the Grimaldi living room. Eve Grimaldi, mother of one of the "rich ladies," had really gone the distance, having bor-rowed, begged or retrieved from her own attic all the silver or silverplate she could find with which to surround these spoiled and worthless women. The "women" themselves were sitting around the room looking slightly disheveled but sa-tiated, having consumed a menu that boggled the mind.

There had been chocolate fondue and strawberries, lady-fingers, banana rounds, jelly beans, "pigs in a blanket," chocolate cigarettes, and a box of After Eight mints. Apart from the tea, the ladies had had the option of several different kinds of soft drinks, served by the mockingly obsequious "maid," Eve Grimaldi, who rolled her eyes and gestured me into the kitchen when I arrived.

"What did they talk about?" I asked.

"Don't ask me," answered Eve. "I'm just the maid. I'd get fired if I blabbed."

I waited with my friend the "maid" while my daughter and her friend Juliane retrieved their various priceless furs and handbags. Finally we left.

"Nobody else's mother came in," complained my daughter once she had gotten into the backseat.

"But I'm a writer," I protested. "All of life is potential material."

"Oh, spare us," groaned my daughter, who had heard me use that line before.

"Well," I persisted, "what did you talk about?" My daughter saw there was no escaping my journalistic probe.

"Oh, we talked about how the youth of today are destroying their minds."

"How?" I inquired.

"By listening to rock groups like the Go-Go's." (My daughter was crazy about the Go-Go's, an all-female teenage band that was cresting at the top of the charts at that time.)

In order to document the deterioration of today's young minds, all the "rich ladies" had listened to the Go-Go's themselves, and everybody had agreed, after listening to each song on both sides of the record, that deterioration was exactly what was going on.

"Do any of the women who were at the tea party have jobs?" I inquired.

"No way!" retorted my daughter. (Jobs were what their husbands had.)

"But we don't know exactly what they do," offered Juliane.

Apparently the husbands of these super-rich-by-marriage wives are more or less shadow figures who flit in and out of their wives' lives, wearing hacking jackets and jodhpurs. If they aren't playing polo with Ronald Reagan, they are out of town. No work for their wives there. In fact, husbands did not surface in the conversation, as it was relayed to me, half as much as the material possessions that their husbands generously allowed them to order from catalogs or ritzy stores that had delivery service.

"Vivi" Charnelle had just installed a bathtub edged with pearls. The maid was being given strict instructions on how to clean it.

Jacqueline Manderly had just fired the butler because he had not shredded the ice before their last cocktail party. Various other domestic problems were raised, discussed and solved.

The main topic, however, seemed to center upon the British royal family. Judging from the names these women had chosen for themselves and their children, England was "in," although the royal family left something to be desired. "They just pay them to be stuck-up," commented my daughter. Prince Charles, everybody agreed, was ruining his life by being married to Diana. Unspoken was the feeling that by marrying Diana, Prince Charles had ruined their own. But all in all, the tea party had been a great success, with plans for duplication in the future. Everyone in attendance felt richer for the experience, which was, of course, the whole point.

PROM NIGHT

~~~~~~

It is happening all over the country. Parents are being screamed at by children who are casting gimlet eyes over front halls that must be shaped up (like their parents) before the doorbell rings. Little brothers, threatening to sabotage their sister's big evening by appearing downstairs in their underpants, are being strong-armed into broom closets. At the last minute, a zipper breaks. ("God's always dumping on me!" wails the victim.) Everyone's emotional inner tube is about to pop. It is the night of the prom.

On this particular night, armies of adolescents march toward each other holding corsages and boutonnieres stapled shut in cellophane. They are excruciatingly nervous, as are their parents, albeit for different reasons. The children are worried, among other things, that their parents might embarrass them. The parents are worried that their children might not return home alive. Who is this boy, lineage and driver's-license status unknown, who is taking out their daughter? Who is this girl—and does she really have a 3 A.M. curfew (as relayed secondhand)—who might corrupt their son?

Before the doorbell rings, parents have been given careful instructions. Answer the bell, turn robotlike on your heels, retreat to the kitchen. Wait there quietly until daughter sings out "Goodbye." Return only to ask the carefully phrased question, "What time should I expect you home?" This last sentence has been renegotiated and renegotiated for several weeks.

Daughter, who is a sophomore, knows that if the answer is later than 1 A.M. that parent will advance like a Spanish duenna with a stiletto on a search-and-destroy mission. Parent knows that daughter's date knows this and will, if he has any brains at all, answer, "One A.M., ma'am." Weeks, perhaps months, of advance psychological and physical preparations have gone into prom night, particularly if you are the parent of a girl.

In this house, we had put the cart slightly before the horse and shopped for the outfit before the escort. This is rather like a writer having an exquisitely flattering photo taken for the dust jacket of a book as yet unwritten, hoping the photograph will give the writer enough inspiration to get to the typewriter or, in this instance, phone. We found an ensemble that struck me as something Lauren Bacall might wear to a funeral in Acapulco. But this is the twentieth century. Girls do not wear net dresses with daisies anymore.

There were problems with my daughter's intended escort. Sam has turned down Sharon when she asked him to her prom last month. Sam might not want to hurt Sharon's feelings by going with my daughter to her prom, or so my daughter's intelligence service informed her. Dozens of telephone calls whipped back and forth across the city as my daughter and her friends discussed the possibility of rejection versus acceptance. We decide to call. Sam says "No." Deep depression ensues. Various neighborhood boys are suggested by her mother. Daughter turns her head to the wall.

Then, from an unexpected corner, comes her older brother to suggest a blind date called from his unpublished but presentable list of friends. Is he goofy-looking or acting?

asks his sister. "Depends," says her brother cryptically. She decides to depend upon his judgment. That was a mistake.

The blind date turns out to be a disaster but that is only the bad news. The good news is that she was rescued at the dance by a fabulous-looking blond six-foot-tall rower (who was at the dance with another girl who was only using him as a cover to see somebody with a Mohawk her parents didn't approve of) who spent the entire evening romancing my daughter. She tumbled home, on time, newly in love and appreciative of God's mysterious ways. I fell asleep thankful that no oak trees had collided with the car that brought her home. One prom down, one to go.

Last year's younger brother in a pair of underpants is this year's Beau Brummell. For his school's dance—on a hired cruise liner—he was approached by not one but two girls from his eighth-grade class who presented him with a package deal. Would he take both of them? Hey, why not?

"What?" I exclaimed incredulously. "You're taking two girls to the school prom?" He nodded, unimpressed with his assignment. They even bought their own tickets. I thought this was taking the twentieth century too far.

My son's first choice of outfits was a rented tuxedo. We called. Fifty dollars. "No way," I replied. His second choice met with my approval—a used-clothing store where you can't carry away all the stuff you can buy with a five-dollar bill.

He emerged with a size 6 woman's black jacket, a waiter's black vest and a silk bow tie (navy blue but who would notice in the dark?). He was scheduled to pick up his dates by 6:30 P.M. He was ready by 3. We killed time. As I drove him across town to pick up his dates, I worried that the parents of the two girls might get the wrong idea about my son. He looked a little like Nathan Detroit or a hit man for the Mafia. We pulled up to Rachel's house and he put on his wraparound sunglasses. Bounding up the front stairs, two bunches of red carnations clutched behind his back, he rang the bell.

Rachel was ready, looking like a young Amy Irving—in her mother's turquoise-blue chiffon dress, bare feet and braces. She was eating a Popsicle. My son did not deserve such melting beauty the first time at bat.

There was more: Brooke, chauffeured to the pickup spot by her mother. Up the stairs came a little blond sunbeam in a blue-sprigged ruffled dress with hair that fell like silk anchored by barettes behind her back. Now we are two beauties, squired by one undeserving, seemingly underwhelmed escort. Yet neither girl seemed to care that they shared. Was this progress? I did not know.

My part in the prom was to pick up all three of them at 10:30 P.M., when the boat would return. I saw them leaning over the railing. My son was spitting into the water. The girls were watching his spit fall, seemingly entranced. The troika was intact.

Falling into the car, all three seemed pleased with the evening. They had had to share the boat with tourists from New Jersey, which took some of the shine out of the starlight. The hot dogs were expensive, but the music was O.K. Everybody had been given cheap fluorescent necklaces, which they dangled out the car windows. By 12:15 A.M. everybody was asleep in his or her own bed.

Had their expectations of the evening been fulfilled? I wondered. Nobody asked or answered that question, although so much romance compressed into so few hours seemed unnatural to me. Next year at this time, I expect that the scenario will be a little more complex. The thought exhausts me. I am getting old.

"I'M PEACHY
NOW"

One morning, while pondering the ways that parents teach
their children to have faith in life, my brain failed me. I
decided, instead, to look for wood. Every fall, with what
little residue of the Puritan ethic remains within me, I make
several sweeps around the neighborhood in search of twigs
and branches. Come winter, we make heavy use of a wood
stove unless we run out of kindling, which I try not to do.

It was a school holiday and the local park was full of
children of all ages: babies packed into strollers, toddlers
hanging by their knees off the jungle gym, and—way off in
the distance sitting on a picnic bench—a teenager staring
into space, listening to a rock song wailing from his tran-
sistor. He was perched on the far edge of childhood, barely
in the park at all.

I gathered wood and thoughts at random, gravitating
toward the tallest trees whose branches had shaken the largest supply of twigs upon the ground. And while I filled up
my arms with fuel, my thoughts turned back to the dilemma of how to give children the sort of hope that will
inwardly support them in moments of despair or darkness.
If parents can be compared to trees, then our beliefs are the

kindling that our children use to start the fire in their lives.

That fire can be doused by a glance from a cab window. Several years ago, my younger son, then eleven, returned from a vacation in Acapulco with his father. The first words out of his mouth were that he was "shocked by the poorness. People there, Mom are so rejected." Specifically, Justin had been driving toward his hotel when he had seen a little boy tied by one ankle to a stake so that he would not stray from the family hut by the roadside. It was the first time my son had felt his own powerlessness, his inability to roll down the cab window, reach out and fix somebody on the other side.

My daughter is currently wrestling with all the complexities of a classmate who is dying of cancer. Less and less does she have the strength to attend school. There are two problems confronting Eliza: how to comfort her classmate, whose courage is, by all reports, extraordinary; and how to do away with her own guilt as she remembers that she had not paid enough attention to her classmate when she was well.

Not only are the battles to have faith in life tested by observing others less fortunate than themselves. My older son, for example, has always had the toughest battles with himself. Born with a more turbulent agenda than the average baby (colic, asthma and, later on, learning disabilities) there were early signs that this was not a human being destined to float like a sunbeam across the waves.

Always he needed more praise than the other two children. Always he needed more structure than I was able to provide. And when he got into trouble, he tended to get into deeper trouble than the other children, which his fiercely private temperament made it difficult for him to acknowledge. Yet when he was twelve years old, I found a note he had scrawled to himself in his bedroom. "God please help me!" I held the scrap of paper in my hand and felt hot wires of helplessness snap around my heart.

Precluded by his stiff resistance to my love, I knew that I could not help him directly. It was a moment when I had completely run out of "kindling" and could only pray for a tree larger than myself to replenish my supply. In that particular crisis it came in the form of a police sergeant in the Second District who befriended my son and asked him to go fishing.

Angels are not as popular as they used to be, except on Christmas cards from the Metropolitan Museum. But too many of them have appeared in human form for me to doubt their existence. I'll say this for angels, however. It is only at my emptiest that they fully unfurl their wings.

There are, of course, many days when life is singing with significance. A fresh fall of snow coinciding with a day off from school and the smell of bacon in the kitchen—these gratuitous moments when all good things come together, as unanticipated as a butterfly landing on a rose, add hope to life when it seems overloaded with pain. Yet now I am speaking, perhaps, more from the adult's perspective. How we teach our children to be on the lookout for hope is, I suppose, dependent upon two things: the child we are teaching and what we, ourselves, think is worth noticing at any given time.

Children often see things we have overlooked. "I saw something pretty beautiful today," said Justin a few weeks ago. "What was it?" I asked. "Fog," he replied matter-of-factly. "It was all mixed up in the trees."

I was reminded, after this report from the world, of a conversation I overheard between a friend of mine and his five-year-old son as we were driving by a country graveyard.

"Daddy," remonstrated the child, "you should hold your breath when you drive by a graveyard."

"Why?" his father asked.

"Because it's polite, since nobody in the graveyard can breathe anymore."

I was charmed by the explanation. His father was not. A long lecture on how human beings decompose after death, turning into various chemicals and gases, ensued, leaving the little boy wide-eyed and silent. We returned to the family's house shortly thereafter and the little boy went into his room to play a record. I heard "My Grandfather's Clock" revised to the following words: "The sun is a mass of in-can-des-cent gas, a gigantic nuclear furnace."

This family was intent upon rearing children according to the latest scientific data. While holding nothing personal against poetry, they did not exactly encourage their children to see "fog all mixed up in the trees."

It could be argued that intimations of beauty and having faith in life are not the same thing. In moments of supreme darkness, butterflies on roses and fog in the trees do not support us. In the darkness, we cannot see these things at all. I agree.

But as a child builds up an inventory of experiences that can be used as proof that life means something (beyond his capacity to see exactly what it means) a parent can have a hand in adding to the child's stockpile of positive information. And perhaps we are the greatest proof, without teaching them anything further, that there is a reason to go on.

In my growing up, I cannot clearly recall my parents. They were background shapes who dished out mashed potatoes and attended school plays. When I asked for something, it was usually given to me. When I sought them out, one or both of them were usually there. And while I did not then see the connection between their presence and my ability to trust in life beyond the immediate family circle, I see it now.

Parents change. We divorce, we remarry, we have careers and aspirations that teach our children that we are not god-like in our immutability, that we can make grievous mistakes, change our minds and lives, too. But if a child's early life is rooted in the knowledge that we are there for him at the beginning, then I think that it is easier for him to absorb changes later on. A parent is a child's first proof that having faith in a power greater than oneself (which is what life is) is justified. And when life reveals itself to be unjust, we can at least witness the paradoxes by their side.

Not long ago, my sixteen-year-old daughter sank into a chair and confessed that she had "had an unhappy childhood." She did not sound particularly sad about it.

"Really?" I answered, feeling a strange ache.

"Really," she confirmed. "I was telling my group leader about it in Europe this summer, and he agreed."

It seemed inappropriate to comment that anybody who has the luxury of "telling my group leader in Europe" about her unhappy childhood was leaving something out of her evaluation, but I was more curious to know, in detail, of what her unhappy childhood consisted. Not that I could revise it now.

My daughter ticked off the reasons and I listened. It was true that the fabric of her life had been slashed a number of times. But as I listened to her explanation I could not control my own unhappiness, or more accurately, self-pity. Granted I wasn't the greatest Brownie leader in the neighborhood, but I did the best I could. Tears involuntarily filled my eyes.

My daughter looked over to where I was silently sitting in consternation.

"What's the matter?" she asked, with obvious sincerity.

"Oh, I guess I am just feeling badly that you think your life was so terrible."

"Don't be sad," she shot back, jumping up from her chair and wrapping her arms around me. "It's not your fault, and anyway"—she backed off and adopted a pose of impish wonderfulness, one hand on her hip—"it doesn't make any difference. I mean, I'm just *peachy* now!"

I looked at my "peachy" daughter and laughed with pleasure. The fog redescended in the tree branches. The butterfly reconnected with the rose.

CAPTURING
THE FLAG

~~~~~~~~~~~~~~~~~~~~~~~~~~~~~~~~~~~~~~~

Last year I received a letter from my college class alumni representative asking me, along with everybody else, to write something about my life since graduation. Our descriptions would then become part of a Twenty-fifth Reunion handbook which would be distributed to all of us when we gathered together to celebrate ourselves en masse. I thought a few minutes and slipped a piece of paper into the typewriter. The following came flowing from the depths of my subconscious onto the page:

Phyllis Grissim Theroux '61, lives in Cobble Creek, Connecticut. The mother of six children, she spends most of her time writing and illustrating children's books, volunteering at the Catholic Workers soup kitchen in Manhattan and helping her husband, Gordon, an architect, work on their country house in Vermont. They have more golden retrievers than they know what to do with. This summer they took the entire family to Europe on a bicycle tour of France, where their oldest child, Thomas, is currently studying history at the Sorbonne.

That was the sort of write-up I once hoped to see under my name after twenty-five years away from college. Life turned out to be more interesting than the above, although the more childish part of me still wishes that it had been possible to purchase the "Cobble Creek" dreamscape like a puzzle in a box which only asked for my patience in assembling it. But nobody interesting I know has had such a life.

It could, of course, be argued that an interesting life is less desirable than a peaceful, bump-free life; you would get no argument from me. I have been dragged toward an interesting life kicking and screaming. Every chance I saw to settle for less, I tried to take. But plot flows toward character, and one has to accept the results of the collision with equanimity if not grace.

I don't know much about grace, except how it feels to be without it, but like many human beings I have wound up having to settle for more of everything—more problems, pain, consciousness and freedom than were on my "wish list" of twenty-five years ago. I wish against wisdom, however, that I could spare my children what I could not spare myself.

We know, at least in retrospect, that most of our heroism is selfish when it comes to our children. We do not want to suffer twice—once for them and again for ourselves—as we watch them stumble around in the dark. We know also that the easy light of childhood has to disappear down a cistern before it gathers itself together and resurfaces later on. We know a lot of things we wish our children did not have to learn. But if there is anything in my life which has given it "interest," it is the realization that my children are separate human beings on separate paths, which, like all human beings before them, they inevitably must travel alone—which reminds me of my younger son.

He disembarked from the bus looking like a fourteen-year-old French dockworker. The felt beret and oversized black wool overcoat that sloshed around his ankles had not been part of his wardrobe three months ago when he left for school.

"Do you notice that I've toned down my appearance?" he asked as we drove home from the bus station.

"I did notice," I answered. His hair no longer rode the crest of his head like an advancing parenthesis. The Iron Cross that used to tug dangerously at one earlobe had been replaced by a discreet wire hoop.

"I feel I've matured," he added.

I cast a glance at the small, chiseled face staring solemnly through the windshield. His eyes were no longer the contemplative eyes of a child absorbing the world without comment. A wind had blown across his consciousness.

"I think you have," I answered, not adding that in the process of his maturing, I had been doing some of my own. There had been no choice.

It is leaving me. The power I once held absolutely over my children's lives is no longer a fat ball of twine in my hand but a fistful of string from the end of the skein. One child no longer lives at home, another is still here but spends most of her time on the telephone plotting new departures, and the third, the youngest child, is away at school for nine months of the year.

There are losses. Never again will I be so physically and emotionally connected to humanity without effort. Those winter mornings when I sleepily stripped a soggy diaper off a shivering child before pulling him into a warm lair of covers to be reheated are gone forever. I can now leave the house without my daughter's flinging herself like a doomed moth against every front windowpane as she tearfully watches me walk down the path. I can return without bracing for three sets of arms and legs wrapped around my torso ("She's back!") in ecstasy. These kinds of losses can feel rather cold.

Then, too, my pronouncements on life are no longer accepted as infallible statements from St. Peter's chair. Often I am not even allowed to complete my infallible statements, even when they are corroborated by *The New York Times*.

"*The New York Times* is full of lies," announced my fourteen-year-old the other morning.

"About everything?" I queried incredulously. "Do you know that *The New York Times* is considered the newspaper of record in this country?"

He blinked, but wasn't going to let my point blunt his. The word "point" as in "What's your . . ." and "That's beside the . . ." has surfaced frequently since my son went away to school and met a boy named Max.

Max, I was told, is so smart he gets high blood pressure just from thinking. Max is teaching my son how to argue. Max has this kit bag full of phrases like "blatantly obvious" and "I rest my case" that my son is busy incorporating into the contents of his own kit bag of devastating comebacks as fast as Max utters them. Around this house, during vacation from school, we were "resting our cases" frequently, although it was "blatantly obvious" that my son was more interested in the sound of his propositions than in their philosophical underpinnings.

"I guess you could say I'm an anarchist-vegetarian, except for hot dogs."

"Nobody's perfect," I replied.

Bypassing the violent aspects of anarchy, which seemed, in my estimation, to be a buzzword for the anarchy of adolescence, I commented that anarchy did not seem to be the philosophy of choice for most people.

"We're still small," he admitted. "But we're growing. I mean, look at me."

I rested my case.

Three years ago, my son the anarchist-vegetarian had been the self-appointed school representative for the Young Republicans, junior division. He wore sports jackets (thereby starting a trend in his parochial school), bow ties, and served Mass on weekdays. For his confirmation name he startled Sister Peggy by choosing the name Jesus, with Luke as a fallback position in case Jesus was shooting too high.

"Well," ventured Sister Peggy, "I suppose your choice is in the right spirit. I mean, we did urge all the boys and girls to pick the name of somebody they admired. But perhaps we ought to check with Monsignor before giving you the go-ahead."

Monsignor had reluctantly approved and I had prayed from the back of the church that the choir would be singing when "Jesus" approached the bishop with his name on an index card. Then I prayed for forgiveness for being so hypocritical. The bishop had done a double-take, glancing over at Monsignor, who had whispered, "Hay-soos," giving the founder of Christianity a last-minute Spanish twist that relieved the bishop's mind of feeling that the name was an act of presumption. That time seems several lifetimes away.

Next year, my son went to a nonsectarian school where you could wash your hair in Jell-O if you wanted as long as you kept up with *The Iliad* in class. It was a very difficult year, exacerbated by some hormones that appeared and others that did not. The pediatrician told my son that she had good news and bad news. He would eventually grow tall but she couldn't say when. My son was only partially mollified.

"Sometimes I feel like I'm waiting to grow the way you

wait in line to get tickets for a movie. I'm afraid that by the time I get to the window they'll be all sold out."

Shortness was compensated for by adopting a straight-up hair style, jack boots with thick soles and "get outta my way" clothing. Once in a restaurant we inadvertently sat next to two of the nuns who had known him in his Young Republican phase. They took one look at him and resolutely lowered their eyes for the rest of the meal, forking through their Caesar salads as if their lives depended upon finding a crouton at the bottom of the bowl. I have often thought that certain parochial schools deserve the name.

Then we were thirteen. I wondered whether I would ever get used to boys using "styling mousse" on their hair. I wondered, more seriously, if the cartoon drawings of people hanging by neckties from shower stalls that I found in my son's room should be taken to heart. A slogan, "Life is for the foolish or the dead," appeared on the cover of a school notebook. "Suicidal Tendencies" is a punk band, but the message of despair was everywhere I looked (including the back of his jeans jacket).

For the better part of that year I kept a very close watch on my formerly sunny, funny, metaphorically inclined child who had turned such a dark eye upon the world. I sought professional help for him and it was appropriate. The verdict was that this was a basically healthy person, but he was in distress, as was I.

Then came a reprieve. For six pine-scented weeks he went away to a summer-camp school where he won all kinds of ribbons for academic excellence and his team consistently triumphed at "Capture The Flag." It was tantamount to putting a sick plant under a Gro-Light. But the next flag he had to capture was ahead of him, on a higher hill. In order to grasp it, he had to let go of me.

✴

My three children are dizzyingly different, one from the other, and sometimes I have felt like a United Nations translator, having to work in three different languages depending upon the child involved.

My older son responds best to simple statements: "I am angry." "You are unhappy." "Please take out the garbage before you leave the house." Analysis is lost upon him; facts he can handle, interpretation of the facts takes more time.

My daughter is a different story. A matter-of-fact, emotionally savvy child who can one minute be shooting nails of reason in my direction and the next minute be collapsing in tears over how "mean people in Poland were to the Jews," she continually surprises me with maxims that delight and take me aback. "Love stinks, Mom, that's rule number one." In moments of vulnerability, she is achingly concise. "Sometimes I think that the only person who understands me is me." The contours of our minds are not similar, but increasingly I have come to be grateful for the differences. Her perspective has widened mine. "We argue a lot," she conceded recently, "but at least it's over important things." Never, in memory, have I had the last word. But often, twelve hours later, I will find that my words were not lost on her. She simply needed time to weigh my words against her own.

The third child could be labeled a soul graft. By instinct, I have known how to deal with him since he was born. Even as an infant, he would occasionally stop nursing and give me an amused look that I interpreted to mean "This is pretty much fun. I wish you could be me." And in many ways that wish was granted. Yet in the separation process that has to take place if the son is to become a man, the wish has to be undone.

This fall when we decided that boarding school would be the logical extension of his triumphant summer-school experience, separation anxieties were not anticipated. I had gone to boarding school at his age and benefited enormously from the barrel hoops of structure that embraced the unsteady staves of my personality. The intuitions of order and beauty I received during that time continue to fuel my imagination. A prolonged exposure to harmony during adolescence is a valuable thing.

There were no tears when I deposited him at the school last September. In fact, I sensed that it would be appropriate if I beat a fairly hasty retreat, once I had seen his room and met the headmaster. Anticipating that I might get physical in his presence among other students at the school, he had instructed me to get any goodbyes over with before we approached the school grounds. "You can kiss me now," he ordered, several blocks away.

The first telephone calls were reassuring. He loved the school, the food was great, and there was a mountain he could see every morning when he woke up that "looks like a bowl of Trix cereal." It had been the right decision. I pictured him hunched over an art tablet near a wood stove in the classroom, away from the mean streets of the city. Apparently they listened to opera during art classes. On his own, he had bought a tape of Haydn's flute concertos. If I ran short of tuition money, I would get a job waiting tables at night to keep him so well.

Then the telephone calls turned slightly anxious. He was developing what he called "the Howard Hughes syndrome," aches and pains in his back, heart and head, which frightened him considerably.

"It's just anxiety," I said reassuringly. "Your mind is reacting upon your body. Is there anything you want to tell me about that might be the cause?"

Sometimes he had a reason: Algebra was difficult, he wasn't doing all that well in French either, and his roommate snored, among other things. We dealt nightly over the telephone with each item as it came up. But beneath the list of particulars I sensed that he was coming generally unraveled. After the school year had shifted from first to second gear, my son was increasingly at a loss as to how to proceed. He was becoming aware of just how far away he was from the family dog.

Finally, it all came out in a 2:30 A.M. phone call that jolted me awake. I heard a weeping voice at the other end. "Mom, I'm afraid I'm going to die."

What do you say to a terrified fourteen-year-old standing in a cold dormitory hall clinging to a lifeline which is only a thin cord that disappears into the wall? Before I uttered a word, I adjusted my tone to that of a compassionate but brisk head nurse.

"Of course you are. Your life hasn't begun and you're afraid it will be taken away."

Oh, the curse of an understanding mother! Even as I said the words and felt a slight relaxation at the other end of the line, I knew that my understanding was, itself, life-threatening. If he was to survive and thrive, he would have to undo the damage I had done to him in the process of understanding him too well. In the transfer of power from parent to child, the child has to learn to understand himself.

The vacation is over. Now we are driving to the airport. I run over his itinerary; he will change planes in Newark, find the taxi I ordered in Albany, and return to school. It was the first time he had negotiated his passage from home to school by himself.

The subject then turned to his "anxiety attacks." He worried that he would have them again, that is, if the plane didn't crash before he got back to school.

"Do you know how you feel when you're just coming out of a movie you had wanted to see?" I asked him. "Sort of bland, satisfied, and uncurious."

He nodded.

"Well, a lot of people feel like that all the time. They're made differently."

"I wouldn't want to be like that," he conceded.

"You don't have a choice. You are who you are. But I can promise you that you won't always have these same fears. Someday you'll be at my end of the telephone talking to one of your children, telling them how you used to feel at their age."

This shift in time and perspective seemed to make sense to him. By giving him a look from my crow's nest into the future, he began to believe in land ahead. At that moment, my car slipped out of gear and we began to lose power. I shifted into a lower one. "I think we'll get to the airport, but I may have to hitchhike home."

I was unprepared for the next shift in time and perspective. "Listen," he said, a more authoritarian timbre in his voice than I had heard before. "If you ever have to hitchhike, Mom, don't ever take a ride from a man—one of those swinging single types could beat you up. So if one of them stops to pick you up, let him go right on by."

"All right," I said obediently.

"Stick with women. Got that?"

"Right."

The trip back to school was not easy. His second flight was canceled, he was put on another an hour later, the man next to him kept predicting a crash, and when he arrived in Albany, his cab had gone. All these mishaps he negotiated.

"I hitched a ride back to school with somebody's grandmother in a pickup truck," he reported later that night.

"Are you feeling fine?" I asked.

"Yup, there was only one bad part."

"What was that?"

"In the pickup truck. I got sort of scared sitting back there alone in the dark."

The image of a fourteen-year-old boy hunched down next to his duffle bag hurtling through the night in the back of a pickup truck lingered in my mind for several days thereafter. We do not easily send our children into the darkness. But it seems to be the only way to the light.